THE EXTRAORDINARY MIND OF AN ORDINARY MAN

Trevor S. Thomas Sr.

CHAPTER 1

This Bug Problem

The day for me had started like almost any other day. I was a newspaper journalist and I had just finished a couple of stories I had been working on. As a writer, my employment was very flexible and most of the work I did was from home. But today I had to leave the comforts of my small, one-bedroom apartment to make a pit stop at the local grocery store to pick up a can of bug spray.

Lately I had been seeing a steady path of ants crawling along the counters in my kitchen, and as much as I wiped the counters clean with bleach and hot water, the ants just kept coming back. My kitchen was always clean so there was no reason to have bugs parading around it like they were. My sink never had more than three or four dirty dishes; since I lived alone, I rarely ever had a sink full of things needing to be washed.

My apartment was small, cozy and inviting. But as inviting as it was, I didn't have company very often. As a matter of fact, at one-point last year, I had not had a single visitor to my home in well over a year. And even then, the one time I did have a visitor, it was only a maintenance man from my apartment complex.

He was in my apartment for pest control, and on that particular day, I just happened to come home while he was there spraying. Seeing a stranger in my home without my permission really bothered me. It bothered me so much that I called the main office and told them to never allow anyone in my apartment if I wasn't there to let them in. I was pretty firm with this demand. Even if it meant I would have to handle the pest control myself, I didn't want anyone in my apartment if I wasn't there.

So, this ant problem probably could have been avoided if I had let the maintenance man handle it, but due to this event it was my problem now. Which is why on this particular day I was headed to the local store for a can of bug spray.

Outside, it had been raining for two days straight and the temperature hovered around 40 degrees. Where I lived this type of weather was typical for this time of year. I lived in a small town called Plymouth, Georgia, about an hour and a half north of Atlanta.

It was a quiet place that had good schools, a low crime rate and a church, seemingly on every corner. In most people's opinion it was a perfect place to live. It was the complete opposite of the hustle and bustle that consumed the mother city of Atlanta just a short way away to the South. I had been living here for several years now and over that time I had grown quite fond of everything it had to offer.

It had a movie theater, a bowling alley, several nice parks, food eateries, an art gallery, a civil rights museum and even a water park that only opened on the weekends. This place had tons of potential, but I rarely took part in any of those activities. I only went out on certain occasions, and when I did go out it had to be for something special.

On those special occasions, I would treat myself to one of the town's best steakhouses. While there, I would order the largest steak on the menu, a butter and sour cream filled baked potato and a large glass of sweet raspberry tea. To me there is absolutely nothing better than a good steak and a glass of sweet tea.

At my job as a newspaper writer, I was always getting recognized for something, although when I first started out that wasn't always the case. In fact, in those early days, I didn't get recognized for anything. It wasn't because I did a bad job, it was because I wrote about things that most people had little interest in.

Things like county school board meetings that had gone awry. Or local efforts to clean up a neighborhood park. Or if there was a new plant coming to town, I was sure to have the inside scoop on how many people they planned to hire.

But most people could care less about the things I wrote about. And I covered ordinary stories like those for several years, until I got my big break. That break came when I wrote a column about a crooked Georgia state senator who received millions of dollars in kickbacks to lobby support to build a new supermax prison. A prison that wasn't needed because of its tremendous cost and also because crime was on a five-year decline.

The new prison cost taxpayers over a hundred million dollars to build, and ultimately led to a huge surge in minority arrests. According to my investigative reporting, arrests in impoverished communities increased sixty percent in one year alone. And as interesting and important as that information was, none of it mattered.

That didn't interest people. That's not what got their attention. What got people's attention wasn't hearing about the skyrocketing cost to build it, or an unjust increase in minority arrests to fill it. Nope. What got their attention, was hearing that a crooked politician had received illegal

4

kickbacks to have it built. And uncovering that fraud propelled my career.

I worked for the Atlanta Journal-Constitution, which at the time was the largest newspaper publication in the South. It had over a million digital subscriptions, and my columns were among the most read and most popular in it. I was what they call a seasoned writer. And that title garnered me a lot of respect and enabled me the privilege to do the majority of my work from home.

But sometimes, like most reporters, I traveled for my work. And when I did travel, I absolutely loved it. I covered interesting and important stories that affected people who lived all throughout the mid, and deep South. That was my targeted area. It was what I called my honey hole for good news.

Which leads me back to this rainy afternoon when I had to pause my work and head to the local grocery store for a can of bug spray. I was planning on going in and picking up something simple, but instead I found something much more complex. I found something far more impactful than a can of bug spray. What I found that day changed my life forever, and I can remember it as clearly as if it happened yesterday.

Chapter 2

A Chance Encounter

When I entered the store, I casually walked to the closest employee and asked them on what aisle I could find the bug spray. I wasn't the type of person who goes to the store for one thing and leaves with ten others. I was focused; I had a plan to be in and out quickly. But when I reached the aisle that had the item I had gone there for, I was puzzled that there were so many products and brands to choose from.

As I stood there reading the labels, picking up and putting down different products, I glanced to my right, and I was immediately caught off guard by what I saw. I saw something special. Very special. Down the aisle from me appeared a woman so beautiful that I had to contain myself to keep from staring. She looked amazing, and she had my absolute full attention.

She wasn't flashy by any means. She was just the opposite. She was casually dressed in hospital scrubs, but they were nicely fitting and showed all of her pristine features. She was a petite, average height, brown-skinned woman who looked to be in her early twenties. Her hair was long and curly, and her skin was smooth and clear. Nothing about her was flashy, but I stood in awe as I watched her from a distance.

She seemed to have a positive energy about her, and I could vaguely hear her softly humming a pleasant tune as she moved down the aisle. And even though she appeared to move hastily, picking up and putting down several products, I could tell she was determined and focused. Whatever it was she was searching for, she was going to find it. And whatever it was she was looking for, luckily for me, it was coincidentally down the same aisle as mine.

As she moved closer to me, I found myself in a slight trance. With each step she took, I became increasingly nervous. I couldn't believe this beautiful woman was coming toward me. I knew I had to do something. I had to say something to get her attention. I wanted her to know that I thought she was amazing.

Maybe I could get her attention by saying hello and introducing myself. Or maybe I could ask her a question, and then introduce myself. I didn't know what to do or what to say, I just knew I couldn't let her pass by without saying *something*.

At the time, I didn't have a girlfriend, or anyone special in my life. I was the definition of a single, ordinary man. I spent most of my time alone, but I was happily married to my work. It was the one thing that brought complete satisfaction to my life.

I wasn't looking for a mate. If I wanted a woman, I could have pursued one. In my line of work, I crossed paths with all types of women. Tons of women. But I never had an interest in any of them like I did for this woman walking toward me. She appealed to me, and before I knew it, she was standing right next to me.

Within seconds we were standing shoulder to shoulder, right next to each other, on the very same aisle. My chest was beating, and my heart was racing. I knew the time to act was now. I knew I had to say something. God knows I wanted to. But as much as I tried to work up the nerve to say something, I just couldn't.

I was so nervous that I couldn't even lift my head up from the can of spray I held in my hand. I wasn't a very outgoing person, and today it really showed. I was a small man in height and stature. I stood about five foot seven, and on a good day I weighed around 150 lbs. I didn't dress in the latest fashions, and nothing about me stood out as someone a woman of her caliber would find attractive.

I had only planned to go to the store for bug spray, so I wasn't dressed in my finest attire. I had on beige knee-high shorts, a tank top that showed my lack of physique and a pair of flip flops that I usually only wear around the house. On top of that, I hadn't been to the barber shop in a month and my hair badly needed to be cut.

So, it was because of those things, and my overall lack of self-confidence, that I couldn't hype myself up to find the words to start a conversation. I wanted to say something, but my mouth just wouldn't allow it. I was pathetic. I couldn't even muster the courage to lift my head from the can of spray I held in my hand to say hello.

As I stood there staring at the can of bug spray, I felt paralyzed. With each second that passed, I knew my opportunity was slipping away, and I couldn't do anything to stop it. And then, to my surprise, after what seemed like forever the woman threw me a lifeline by asking me a question.

Our conversation went as such:
"Do you know if this can of spray is any good?" she asked.
"I'm not sure, but I think they all kinda do the same thing," I replied.

8

"Well, I'm trying to find something that doesn't have a strong odor. I don't like it when you spray and then the smell is so strong you have to leave the room."

"Yeah, I know what you mean," I said.

"So what kind of problem do you have? What are you trying to get rid of? I hope it's not roaches, because I absolutely hate roaches." she said.

Then she smiled at me, and her smile was amazing. When I looked into her eyes, I felt a soothing energy. I was absolutely blown away by how pretty she was. She was beautiful, and on top of that, she seemed to be very friendly and outgoing, and when I looked at her, I couldn't help but smile.

But as much as I enjoyed looking at her, I almost couldn't. Because when I did, I found myself blushing and smiling uncontrollably. I had to look down and away from her to keep my composure. I felt like I was blushing too much and smiling way too hard.

I thought if I didn't look away, she would surely think I was strange. Or at the least very immature. I was blushing like a teenager, and I couldn't help it. This woman made me nervous. But I liked the way I felt. I liked the nervousness that possessed me. And fortunately for me, as our conversation continued my nerves slowly began to ease.

I said, "No it's not roaches, it's ants. They all over my kitchen counter. I'm not sure where they coming from but I'm tryna find something to get rid of them. I hope this can does the trick."

Then she said, "I have them in my garage but sometimes they get in my house."

Showing me the can of spray she held in her hand she continued, "This seems like something that might work. What do you think?"

9

Looking at the can of spray she held up, I put down the one I was holding and picked up one like she was showing me. Then I read the back label aloud.

"Well, this says it's odorless and kills on contact. I think this might be good. This should do the job."

"Well, I sure hope it does," she said.

"I'm sure it will," I replied.

"Well how can you be so sure?" she countered.

Then I said, "Well dang, what kinda ants you got over there?"

I said this while laughing sarcastically. I made it seem as if she had ants that were resistant to bug spray or a type of radioactive ant that couldn't be killed with ordinary over-the-counter products. She just laughed and began to smile. And as she smiled, I smiled. And as she laughed, I laughed. We had definitely made a small connection.

"Well, I got regular ants just like everybody else," she said teasingly, "what you tryna say? What *I* was saying was… you said you were sure this would work. I'm sure it will too. But what if it doesn't? How can I get in touch with you to let you know if it doesn't work?"

And then she blushed and smiled at me again, and I knew exactly what she was doing. She was asking me for my phone number. I couldn't believe my luck. To meet this beautiful woman and then have her ask me for my number. What were the chances of that? She was taking the lead again and I was really glad she did.

After I gave her my number, she called my phone from her phone and told me to save her name and number. She told me her name was Diana Johnson and said she would call me later that evening to let me know if the bug spray, I recommended had worked.

I couldn't believe how cool this was. Here I was in the grocery store exchanging numbers with this beautiful woman

10

after a brief conversation about bug spray. I was curious to see where this would go. When I left the grocery store, I felt renewed. It was an absolutely great feeling. I was anxious to talk with her again, and later in the evening I would get my chance.

I hurried home to prepare myself for her call. She said she would call me later that evening, but that was several hours from now. So all I could do was sit on my couch and wait. And waiting I did. I must have glanced at my phone and checked my ringer three, four, maybe five times. I didn't want to miss her call.

I couldn't wait to talk to her. I was so nervous. I still couldn't believe how everything played out. I felt like the luckiest man alive.

When the clock hit seven-thirty, it had been three hours since I had spoken with her at the grocery store. I had already sprayed my kitchen counters and killed all the ants that had been parading across them. The product I bought, and had recommended for Diana, worked exactly as advertised. It not only killed the ants, but it was also odorless, and that was something Diana said she really wanted.

As I waited for her call my nerves were unsettling. To prepare myself for our conversation I wrote down as many things as I could think about that we could potentially talk about over the phone. I wanted to be prepared, and I definitely wanted to seem interesting. I wanted to make sure we could have a conversation that covered more than just the ant problem in her garage and on my kitchen counters. Here's what I wrote down:

1. What do you do for a living?
2. Where are you from?
3. How old are you? I wasn't sure if this was a good question. I was always told never to ask a woman her

age. But I thought this rule only applied to older women and she definitely wasn't old, so I put a check mark next to it. I figured it would be okay to ask.

4. Do you have any children?
5. What things interest you?
6. Are you in a relationship? This was another question that I had a problem with, so I planned to save it for last. I didn't want to ask her this and then have her say yes. That would give her an easy out and could possibly end our conversation before it even started. If she was in a relationship, I didn't want to know about it. Not now, cause it didn't matter. She approached me so maybe she was interested in me. The way she smiled and blushed at me, I knew she was interested. Plus, she asked for my number. So, I wasn't going to ask that question. Nope, not that one.

Then at 8.30 p.m., after several long hours of watching the clock and writing down and going over my talking points, the call finally came. It was her. It was Diana Johnson.

When I looked at my phone, I knew it was her. At the grocery store she asked me to save her name and number in my phone, which I did. So when I answered my phone, knowing right it was her, I tried to be a little comical. I answered my phone and said, "Hello Ms. Diana… hello Ms. ants in her garage lady."

Then she laughed and replied back, "I know you didn't just call me the ant lady." At which we both laughed back and forth. Again and again, we laughed. It was a great feeling. I could feel tons of positive energy on the other end of the phone.

I could feel her smiles, her laughter and all of her positive vibes. And I could tell she was smiling because I was smiling too. And as our conversation continued, I was blushing hard over the phone. Part of me felt that on the other end of the phone, Diana was blushing too. We had a great conversation and talked for what seemed like an eternity.

But we were mostly laughing, smiling, and welcoming each other's comments. Our conversation was so smooth that I didn't even need my talking points. The paper that I wrote down my talking points on lay neglected on the coffee table. I hadn't looked at it even once. I didn't need to. We had a strong connection and our conversation flowed. We talked about all kinds of things.

But our chance encounter at the grocery store received the least bit of discussion. Outside of me calling her the ant lady, I don't remember us talking about ants or bugs at all. Not one time. We dipped and dabbed in a number of topics, and I can't remember half the things we discussed. But the one thing I did remember was that we both agreed to meet again. We agreed that our conversation deserved the right to continue.

So we arranged to meet the next day at a local Starbucks. This time to sit down and talk. We planned an in-person, sit down conversation. And as our phone call ended, it was clear that we both enjoyed speaking to each other and we both looked forward to chatting again. When I hung up my phone, I was already anxious for the next day. I didn't know if this was a date or a follow up conversation, but whatever it was I looked forward to it.

Chapter 3

Group Homes

The next day I finished up some of the writing that I had been working on and headed to the local Starbucks. We decided that 5 p.m. was a good time to meet since it allowed her time to go home after work to take care of a few things and then head over afterward. I was anxious, so I arrived at Starbucks about fifteen minutes early and to my surprise, Diana was already there.

When I walked in, I found her seated at a table next to the door. She had a small book in her hand that she was reading. When she saw me, she immediately put the book down and waved me to her table. After I sat down, she smiled at me and told me she had just gotten there a few minutes before I did. And after our brief welcome chat, our conversation picked up almost immediately from where it left off the night before.

She was smiling and I was smiling again, but unlike yesterday where I found myself blushing like a teenager on a first date, today I was calm. Today I was composed. Today I was relaxed. And Diana was too. Not only was she relaxed, but she was also very attentive.

She noticed that my fingernails had not been clipped and asked me how often I cut them. Then she asked me how often I cleaned behind my ears, how often I did my laundry, how often I washed my car and a barrage of other questions.

It almost seemed like she had written down a list of talking points like I had done the previous night.

Some of the questions she asked me would make some people feel uncomfortable, but I welcomed them all. They made me feel appreciated. Just hearing her ask me questions, and knowing she had an interest in me, made me feel good. I felt wanted and that was a good feeling to have.

Initially, I didn't ask any questions. I just answered the questions she asked me. I was enjoying her company and I was all smiles. But then, about fifteen minutes into our meeting, our conversation shifted from meet and greet type questions, to questions with much more substance. Questions that required a lot more thought, honesty, and a lot more details.

It started when I asked Diana about her family. When speaking of them she became somewhat subdued, serious and focused and I could tell this was a topic she definitely wanted to talk about.

It was clear that her family meant a great deal to her and talking about them seemed almost therapeutic. She spoke honestly and freely, and as she talked, I listened attentively. And once she got really comfortable with me, and completely settled in, her story took off and pulled me in.

She said, "Well, I was an only child, and I had a very unique childhood. My mother raised me until I was sixteen years old. Then she died suddenly of an illness. After her death I was sent to live with my grandmother who I did not have a previous relationship with.

"My mother was a beautiful person, and I favored her a lot. And although she caught the eyes of many men, she stayed single, and devoted all of her time to me, making sure I had a good life. And she did a good job at it.

"I loved my mother, and we did almost everything together. And we would talk about everything. But she never talked much about her childhood. I knew almost nothing about any of my relatives. The only relative I knew of was my grandmother. But before I was sent to live with her, I rarely ever saw her, and I never heard from her.

"When my mother died, me having to live with my grandmother was the most disappointing experience of my life. I was miserable. My grandmother rarely spoke to me, and she wasn't interested in getting to know me. When I lived with her, she spent most of her time in her bedroom, locked away reading her Bible or listening to old gospel music.

"We didn't communicate at all. And although we lived together, I had to do everything for myself. My grandmother was very strict. I wasn't allowed to watch TV at night. I wasn't allowed to go out with friends. I wasn't allowed to have boys call the house, and I wasn't allowed to talk on the phone after 6 p.m.

"After school I had to come straight home. If I was late, I was grounded. When I came home, I did my homework, I heated up something to eat, watched TV until 8 p.m. and then I went to bed. Every day. Every night. I followed the same routine.

"My bedroom didn't have a TV or a radio. The only TV we had in that whole house was in the living room. For my grandmother, sinful shows came on after eight. So at 8 p.m., that's when I went to bed. Every day, every night. It didn't matter if it was a Monday or a Sunday. I was in bed by 8 p.m.

"But when I went to bed, I rarely ever went right to sleep. I would lay in my bed, close my eyes, and try as best I could to dream about my mother. I missed her so much. I went from being loved and cared for, to being unwanted and neglected. I thought about my mother every night.

"You can't imagine how alone I felt, and how sad I was. I didn't know how, or why I was in my situation, but I longed for my mother. And at night I tried as best I could to connect with her. I tried to find her soul.

"When I laid in my bed I prayed as hard as I could. But I didn't pray to God, I prayed to my mother. I prayed *for* my mother. I prayed for her to come to me. I prayed for her to appear in my dream, to hug me and hold me and tell me she loved me.

"I needed to feel her energy, and I wanted her to appear in my dream. I missed her dearly. I just wanted to see her one more time.

"So, every night, I did the same thing. I prayed to my mother and then I meditated. Prayer and meditation, and then *more* prayer and *more* meditation. I did this faithfully every night.

"And then one night, my prayers were answered. My mother came to me. She heard and answered my call. When she appeared in my dream, she was as beautiful as I remembered. She was even more beautiful than before she passed.

"She came up to me, held my hand, and walked with me. While we walked, she told me she loved me and that she missed me. She told me how sorry she was that she couldn't be here for me. We were both so sad. And then she turned and faced me.

"She looked me in my eyes and told me it was time for me to move on. She said it was time for me to focus on what I have and not what I had. And I understood. I knew what she was saying, and what I had to do. I had to move on.

"But before she left, she said something else. She told me that I was not alone. She said one day they will come for me; they will love me, and they will protect me. And then she left. My dream ended and my mother was gone.

"And when I awoke, I felt much better. I felt at peace and could finally rest easier at night. After that dream, which was the last time I prayed to my mother. Now I never stopped thinking about her, but that was the last time I meditated and prayed for her.

"After that dream I took the cards, I was dealt, and I played with them. I accepted the fact that I was on my own. But I would never get over what she told me. Not that it was time for me to move on. I understood that. I never forgot when she told me I was not alone and that one day they would come to me and protect me and love me. I didn't know what that meant, and to this day I still don't. But whoever 'they' were, they never came."

As I sat there and listened to Diana, I could feel the sorrow in her voice. This same beautiful woman who just minutes ago was blushing with joy and full of energy… she was now defeated and sad. But in spite of how painful it was for her to discuss the loss of her mother she kept talking.

She had a story to tell, and I was there to listen. I was her audience. She didn't want or need a response; she just needed an ear. And as Diana continued talking, her story of isolation further touched my heart, and drew me even closer to her.

She continued, "Living in my grandmother's house, I longed for a friendship. I felt so unappreciated around her. I felt like a mere stranger to whom she had offered a place to stay. She didn't feel like family, and her home never felt like my home. There was no love. It was just a place where I lived. It was never a place I called my home.

"And my grandmother didn't want me to feel comfortable. She rarely bought me new clothes, sneakers or anything that would have made me fit in at school. I wore hand-me-down clothes from thrift stores. My hair was always neat, but it was never styled. I never had any money and I rarely talked to people at my school. It wasn't because I was shy, but because I just didn't fit in. I didn't have what they had, so I chose to stay by myself.

"My grandmother was certainly not poor, but I dressed poorly at school. My clothes were always clean, but they were old and dated. I didn't have money to buy anything, and the only new clothes I got were the ones she brought home after our church had a clothing drive, or whatever clothes she found on sale at the local thrift store. Those were the only new clothes I got to wear.

"So, I wore those old clothes and stuck to myself. I was alone at home and at school. But then one day my feelings of loneliness temporarily disappeared after I met a young man at my school. He wasn't the most handsome guy, but he took an interest in me. And I really liked that because, other than my mother, nobody showed me any attention. So I welcomed him and the attention he gave.

"He would smile at me in class, sit next to me in the cafeteria, and he would walk me to the bus after school. He was a really nice guy, and at some point, I started to like him. I liked him so much that I decided it was okay to be with him. Not just mentally but physically. So, we got together, and I gave him the one thing I had that was special to me. The one thing I had that was truly mine.

"And he was a perfect gentleman. We only did 'it' once and he was cool. He was special to me because he made me feel special. But unfortunately, our perfect romance, and my perfect gentleman, weren't so perfect, because I ended up getting pregnant.

"At first, I was scared, and he was too. Neither one of us wanted a child. We were both only sixteen, and there was no way we could take care of a child.

19

"He tried to help. He told his older sister about it, and she said she would help me if I wanted to get an abortion. She said she knew a doctor that would do it and my grandmother wouldn't have to find out. He and his sister were hoping I would get an abortion and end my pregnancy. But deep down inside I knew I couldn't. I knew I would never do that.

"And when I told him I was keeping my baby he called me stupid and selfish and a bunch of other mean words. After he said those words to me, I stopped talking to him and he stopped talking to me. I would see him at school, and he would walk right by me as if I was a total stranger. Here I was carrying his child, and he wanted nothing to do with me or his baby.

"I tried to hide my pregnancy as long as I could. But eventually my grandmother found out. And when she did, I was told I had to leave. I had to leave her home. She said I was no longer welcome, and that I was an embarrassment to her. She said she would not allow a teenaged heathen to bring sin into her home.

"She said she would talk to her pastor and then the Lord (and in that exact order) and afterwards, she would let me know what they told her to do with me. The next day when I returned home from school, my grandmother had packed all of my belongings and put them in one large trash bag in the living room. Everything I owned was in that bag and seeing it there in the middle of the living room, made me realize just how small and insignificant I was.

"There were also two members of the church standing with her in our living room. One was deacon Johnson, and the other was his wife, Theresa. They told me they were taking me to youth services. They said I didn't have to worry, and that they would make sure I got there safely. So that was

20

it. I said goodbye to my grandmother, and I left that chapter of my life, forever.

"Youth services placed me in a group home for pregnant teens, and I stayed there until I had my baby. After I had my baby, they moved me to another group home for teenage moms. And I really liked it there. The girls were cool, and we all bonded. The staff there seemed to really care about us. They watched our kids while we went to school and were always nice to us. And they even watched the kids of some of the older girls, so they could take college classes during the day.

"We were all told we could stay there until we turned twenty-one. That was when we would age-out and no longer qualify for housing. Some of the girls stayed there all the way up till they turned twenty-one. I don't know where they went once they turned twenty-one, and I vowed I wouldn't be there long enough to find out.

"When my baby was born, it was a son, and I named him Isaac. I made a promise to him that I would do everything I could to make sure he had a good life. So, I finished high school, got my diploma and then I went to nursing school. Once I finished, I got a job as a nurse and moved out of the group into my first apartment.

"I will never forget the girls I met in those group homes. They came around at a time in my life when I needed someone the most. A time when I needed friends. And they were good friends.

"So, there we were. Me and Isaac in this big ole world. Just the two of us. No one to rely on and no one to turn to but each other. He needed me and I needed him. And the pieces in my life were finally starting to fall together.

"Then one day I received a call from an attorney. The attorney told me that my grandmother had passed and that the home she owned and lived in for the past forty years had been left to me. He said no other relatives were listed in my grandmother's will. No one but me, Diana Johnson.

"All I needed to do was confirm my identity and then the house was mine, free and clear. No mortgage, no delinquent taxes, no liens, no loans. Nothing. Nothing but a house. The house my grandmother kicked me out of was soon to be mine.

"So just like that, my life had changed again. At first, I resented the fact that my grandmother, a woman who threw me out on the streets and treated me like a virus, had left me her home. This same unloving woman added my name to her will and left me the only thing she valued. I was confused and I was angry, and I couldn't understand why. But later I realized I never knew her, and I would never know her ways.

"Over time I came to accept that, for whatever reason unknown to me, my grandmother left me her home. I imagined it could be a place where I could raise Isaac. A place where we could create our own memories. A place we could fill with warmth and love, and a place that we could cherish. A place that one day I might possibly leave to him.

"So yep, my life changed again. I packed all of my things from my small one-bedroom apartment and moved them into my grandmother's house. But this time it was not just a house, it was a home. It was my home. My home on 910 Blue Heart Lane."

Hearing Diana tell her story was an amazing experience. I could tell she had been through a lot, and also overcame a lot. I could tell that she was more than just a beautiful face. She was a beautiful person. She then talked a bit more about her home on Blue Heart Lane and I continued to listen.

"Well, my house on 910 Blue Heart Lane is not a very big house. It's small, but it's nice and cozy. It has three bedrooms and two bathrooms and sits on a quiet street. Most of the people who live on my street are older. And like my grandmother, they have lived in their homes for many, many years.

"With so many older people, there weren't many kids in our neighborhood for Isaac to play with. And the last thing I wanted to do, is have him confined to his home like my grandmother did to me. So, I created a schedule that would keep him busy. A schedule that was easy for both of us to follow. One we've been following for a few years now.

"Mondays, after work I go grocery shopping at Publix. That's why you saw me there yesterday. I always go shopping on Monday. Nothing heavy. I just pick up a few things we're running low on at the house. Things like milk, cereal, detergents, and a few other items. And Isaac stays in the afterschool program on Mondays. They let the kids run for hours and he really likes that.

"Tuesdays, believe it or not, I come here every Tuesday. I come to this same Starbucks to read and relax. I like coming here because no one bothers you. I can order a cup of coffee and sit here as long as I want. And Isaac goes to the afterschool program again on Tuesdays.

"Wednesdays, I pick up Isaac from school and we go to the library. I let him pick any book he wants and then I let him read to me. After that I read it back to him. I don't know who likes to read more, me or Isaac, but we both love to read.

"Thursdays, I go to the gym after work to get a little cardio in. I try to work out once a week. I gotta keep myself healthy. And Isaac gets picked up after school by the YMCA. They have an after-school karate club, and he really likes going to that.

"On Fridays, I let Isaac ride the bus home from school. His bus stop is at the end of the street. Sometimes I'll go down there and greet him and the other kids when they get off the bus, and other times I'll let him walk down the street by himself. It makes him feel independent. See, I take him to school every day, and Friday is the only day he gets to ride the school bus. He really likes riding the bus and walking home by himself. And on weekends we don't have anything planned. Me and Isaac just play it by ear.

"Okay, so I feel like I've been talking too much. Now it's your turn. Tell me something about yourself. I know you're a journalist but what do you like to do? What interests you? When you're not writing stories or covering news, what do you do?"

And so I replied to her question by saying, "Well, writing is kinda what I do. It's what interests me. If I'm not writing, I'm bored. All my life, I've been writing stories. Short stories, long stories, actual and fictitious. Helping people get their voices heard is what motivates me. When I started working for the newspaper it was the most rewarding job I ever had. It actually doesn't feel like a job to me. It's something I would do for free. I love it."

"Wow. That's pretty cool," she replied, "so how did you get that job? How did you get your foot in the door?"

And I said to her, "Actually I got my foot in the door when I was in high school. My senior year I entered a writing contest at my school. My English teacher handed out flyers to all her students. The Atlanta Journal-Constitution was doing a short story contest for high school seniors all over the state. The winner would get one thousand dollars, and have their story appear on the front page on their Sunday edition."

"Really? So, what happened?" she said.

"I had to write a short story in five hundred words or less. Which is about one full page. So, I submitted my story and I won," I said.

"So… what was it about? You gotta be more specific than that. I just shared a twenty-minute mini biography with you. You gotta open up. Tell me the details, what did you write about?" she asked.

"Okay. Well, I wrote a short story titled *How Adam and Eve Lost Paradise.*"

"Wow, this should be interesting," came her reply, "now we are getting somewhere."

Chapter 4

Adam and Eve

"In my story, Adam was a farmer who had a large and plentiful garden, and his garden bordered a big and beautiful lake. Adam had everything he could ever need and went wanting for nothing. He loved his garden, and he worked in it every day. But one day, while he was working, something came over Adam. He became visibly upset and started to cry.

"The clouds (who witnessed everything) saw Adam crying, and immediately told God. When God heard of it, he asked Adam why he was crying. God said, 'Adam, my son, haven't you got everything your heart desires? You have a plentiful garden with all the foods you can eat. You have everything. Why do you cry?'

"And then Adam replied and told God that he was lonely. He thanked God for his garden but wanted someone to share it with. Someone to work in the garden with him. So, God satisfied Adam's request, and the next day he sent him a woman named Eve.

"She would work with him in his garden and keep him company. But in return for Eve, God gave Adam one order. An order that he said must be obeyed. His order was that neither he nor Eve, no matter how hot it was, neither of them were ever allowed to swim in the forbidden lake."

"This is getting interesting. I'm liking how this is going," interjected Diana.

And so I continued, "Well one day it was really, really hot outside and Eve begged Adam to take a swim in the forbidden lake. She pleaded with him, crying to Adam, 'I just want to cool off. It's just so hot. Please let me cool off in the lake. I won't stay for very long.' Adam told her no and she cried to him again, 'please Adam, please let me swim.' But Adam was obedient to God and refused her request. He had no plans to break God's order.

"Well at first Eve complied and did as she was told. But later, when Adam was out of view, she defied God's order and jumped into the lake. And while she was swimming, she cut her foot on a large rock on the bed of the lake. Eve was in a great deal of pain, so she screamed loudly. She screamed so loud that the clouds heard her and immediately went and told God.

"God was very upset and harshly punished Adam and Eve for what had happened. The bleeding on the bottom of Eve's foot eventually stopped, but God told her she would continue to bleed for nearly half her life. He told her that as a constant reminder of her disobedience, she would bleed once a month through a biological cycle.

"And God punished Adam as well. Adam would be punished for his lack of wisdom. He was being punished for his inability to find a way to keep Eve from swimming in the lake. Adam had long beautiful hair that came to his shoulders. He would often twist his hair with his fingers to create powerful dreadlocks that symbolized strength. Over time, Adam's hair would recede, and he would eventually go bald. Losing all of his hair and the prestige that came with it. And that's it. That's basically how it went. That was my story."

Then Diana chimed in and said, "That is an amazing story. How did you come up with that? You are super creative. I could never think of anything like that."

27

To which I explained, "As a writer that's what I do. Thoughts come to my head, and I write them down. I have tons and tons of stories I've written and most of them are way better than that. I wrote that a long time ago in high school."

Diana replied, "Okay, so first let's go back. How did this story get your foot in the door with the Atlanta newspaper? And then… well I have a bunch of other questions, but let's just start with that."

I said, "Well, not only did I win the contest and the thousand dollars, but my story was featured in the newspaper. Just like they promised, my high school short story was on the front page of the Atlanta Journal-Constitution. And I got tons and tons of praise. Everybody that read it loved it. They all loved my story.

"Well not long after, I got a call from a dean at Columbia College. They offered me a full scholarship to their school of journalism. I gladly accepted it. And then when the Atlanta Journal-Constitution heard about my scholarship, they offered me a job once I finished school. And that's how I got my big break. I got my foot in the door from a story I wrote when I was in high school."

"That's amazing!" exclaimed Diana, "I'm surprised that things fell into place like that, and I'm so happy for you. I'm glad you're able to do something that you love. I'm a nurse and I like my job, but I don't love it. So, what else have you written? I would love to read your work."

I replied, "I've written a bunch of stuff. But most of the things I write are about my life experiences. My own personal experiences. I had a lot of crazy and tragic things happen in my life, and I wrote about some of them. They aren't necessarily things I would wanna share with the public, but things I kinda wrote for therapy."

Diana added, "I understand. But a lot of writers write about crazy and even tragic things in their lives. Look at Maya Angelo. She's a great example. And then look at Malcolm X. He had a ton of tragedy in his life. I think you should share your stories with the world. And if you don't want to start with such a big audience, maybe you could start with me. I'm a great listener. What about your family? Let's start with them. I told you about my family, now tell me about yours."

I replied, "Well... I have a small family. Growing up it was just me, my mom and dad and my sister April. My sister was much older than me. Seven years to be exact. But even though she was older than me, she was cool. She wasn't the type of sibling to disown me cause I was younger than her. She was different. She wasn't like that.

"She really looked out for me. Whenever I needed her, she was there. I would have loved to have had a brother, but if I had a choice between one of them and my sister, I would absolutely keep her. Cause she was really cool. And growing up, she always looked out for me.

"My parents were cool too. My mom was like the best mom a kid could have. She wrapped her arms around our family and showed us how to love each other. She showed us what it meant to be a family. That was all she cared about. Making sure we were taken care of and had the things we needed. All my friends loved my mom. She was different from the moms they had.

"One of my friends' moms drank too much and was always cussing and fussing. Every time I went by his house, if she was home, she was drinking. And if she was drinking, she was going after people. He hated seeing his mom drunk all the time but there wasn't anything he could do about it.

"And another one of my friends' mothers was never home. She worked like three jobs and he and his brothers practically raised themselves. And that wasn't good. His dad wasn't around, and he never saw his mom. But he loved coming over to my house. If nothing else but to have a home-cooked meal or eat a piece of my mom's homemade apple pie.

"Not all my friends' moms were bad moms. Some of them just weren't as good as mine. And I was blessed to have a great dad too. My father worked at the auto plant for as far back as I can remember. He was gone a lot for work, but we saw him enough to know he loved us.

"And then we lost him when I was in high school. That was a sad chapter of my life, but we got through it. My mother pulled my sister and I closer to her than we were before and loved us as hard as she could. And her love made it easier for us to handle his passing.

"My father taught us lessons of life, and my mother taught us the value of love. Between the two of them, we had everything we needed. As a kid, I didn't miss anything. Only thing I ever wanted was to be a kid forever. Being a kid was easy but growing up was tough. It was very tough."

Diana replied, "Oh wow. That's just terrible. I'm so sorry to hear that. I hate that you had to share that. I didn't want you to have to relive those feelings. I'm sorry about that. I know you must miss your dad. He seemed like a good man."

I said, "He was. My childhood is filled with events like that. Had I not lived through some of them I wouldn't believe they happened. Some of the things were traumatic and some were mystic and mind-boggling. Some were certainly book worthy while others were not.

"I did, however, have one experience that I wrote about. It's tragic, but I think it's the best story I have ever written, *and* it's a real-life experience. But that's not a story I can verbally share with you. It's way too lengthy to discuss.

It's much more detailed than what happened to my father. That was an event that I experienced firsthand, and it changed my life forever."

Diana said, "Well you don't have to tell me about it. If you already wrote it, email me a copy. I would love to read it. And I promise you after I read it, I won't share it or discuss it with anyone."

"Okay," I responded, "but I'm not worried about that. It was a major event in my life that's been written about many times. You may have heard about it. But I'll email it to you anyway. It's a powerful story and I think it's something you will enjoy reading."

"Well now you really have my attention," said Diana, her face full of interest, "I'm super curious. I didn't know I was sitting here with a famous person. Someone people have written about. Wow!"

"Lol," I smiled, "I am definitely not famous. I just was a part of something big and I have my version of the events. That's all."

Then Diana interrupted me and said, "So here is my email address. I'm writing this down for you, so you don't forget to send me a copy. I wanna read your work, and I'm gonna be very disappointed if you don't send it."

Diana wrote her email address on a piece of paper that she pulled from her purse. Our conversation was excellent. We had both really enjoyed talking about our experiences and things were going great between us. As she was writing her email down, she asked me another question about my childhood.

"So earlier you mentioned there are things in your childhood that were mystic. Can you tell me about that?" she said, "I love mysteries. I used to love *the X files* and *unsolved mysteries*. Whatever happened to those shows anyway?"

I replied, "I'm not sure about the TV shows, but my story is kinda long. It might take me a few minutes to tell you. But it's pretty cool. Are you ready for it?"

And Diana said, "Yes sir. Let me hear it. I'm all ears."

Chapter 5

Grandma's House

I said, "Okay. So, growing up, one thing I will always remember was going to my grandmother's house for Memorial Day. It was the one day in the entire year, when the whole family got together and just had a great time celebrating being a family.

"This was the day when you saw your aunts, uncles, and cousins who you haven't seen for a whole year. Now we had family reunions mind you, but those were like every other couple of years. But every year, no matter what, we always made our way to my grandmother's house for Memorial Day.

"She lived in a small home in the country down a long dirt road. As a kid I remember as soon as we got outta the car, the first thing we did was hi-five and hug our cousins who we hadn't seen all year. After that... we just ran and ran and chased each other and enjoyed being kids.

"You could run through the woods, or you could run down the long dirt road. If you didn't want to do that, you could run circles around my grandmother's house. There were plenty of places to run and we ran and hid in all of them.

"I remember how as the kids ran around the house and in and out of the woods, our fathers, and uncles and all of the other men would get the barbecue grills going. While at the same time, all the women prepared and organized the items needed for our big yearly picnic.

"We always had plenty of food, and all the grape and peach sodas you could drink. I thought the best part was lighting the fireworks and firecrackers when the sun went down. But way before that, once everyone arrived, the women would start to gather the children into the cars parked all up and down the long dirt road.

"When we heard someone yell out, 'hey... y'all come on down here... we're getting ready to go.' We all came running. And just like that, in from the woods we came, and found our way into the back seat of one of the many cars lined all the way down the long dirt road.

"Our tradition had officially begun. My grandmother started this tradition many years ago, and it's something we all looked forward to. While the women and children loaded into cars, my grandmother slowly made her way to the pace car that would lead the pack. She was our escort. Leading everyone to our Memorial Day destinations.

"And as we headed out, we would wave goodbye to the men who would stay behind and prepare the food we would feast on when we returned. With all the women, children and elders packed tightly in every available car, we headed out on our yearly ritual. Our first stop was Greenway Cemetery.

"You see, a big part of our tradition was that we drove to the cemeteries of each of our loved ones who had died and were buried in the area. It didn't matter if they died last year, or if they died twenty or thirty years ago, we paid a visit to the grave sights of all our family members who were buried around town.

"From what I can remember, we must have driven to three, four or maybe even five different cemeteries throughout the city. And at every one of them my grandmother would tell the story of the person who was buried there. She would tell us who they were, how we were related, how they died and who they left behind.

"I was amazed that she knew so much about all these people, and how knowledgeable she was of our entire family. Not only did she know everyone, but she knew something important about each person. She knew something special about each member of our family who had passed away.

"As she spoke, she painted a visual picture of each of our deceased family members while we all stood closely together and listened. Listening as my grandmother introduced us to what I called 'the art of storytelling.' She was an absolutely great storyteller.

"When she wanted you to feel sad, you felt sorrow. When she wanted you to feel good, your face would light up with a smile. I remember she would say 'here lies your aunt so and so, and over here lies your uncle Joe and Moe.' Lol.

"I didn't know any of those people, and I wasn't particularly interested in hearing their life stories. But I must admit, I did find it interesting hearing how some of them had died. I will never forget those stories.

"We had two eleven-year-old twin cousins who died in a car accident. We had an uncle who was stabbed to death in a bar fight, a three-year-old baby cousin who was killed by a stray bullet, and a teenaged cousin who committed suicide.

"We had a bunch of relatives who died in all kinds of ways. But most of the people were old relatives who died peacefully of old age. I liked hearing their stories. They all were interesting. But none of these people's life stories or deaths caught my attention like that of a distant cousin who had died a few years ago.

"She was only thirteen years-old when she died. But she didn't just die, she was murdered. My grandmother said

35

she was kidnapped and then killed after walking home from a friend's house.

"Sadly, she took a familiar shortcut through the woods. But that time-saving gamble ended up costing her life when two homeless men, high on drugs, saw her alone in the woods and viciously attacked. She didn't stand a chance and sadly she would never be seen alive again.

"Her story was a sad one and that touched us all. Not just because of how she died, but also because of how my grandmother told her story. While speaking of the sorrows of this child's life, my grandmother reached into her purse and took out a small folded up picture of our young cousin.

"After she unfolded it, she passed it around for everyone to see. My grandmother was especially touched by the loss of this child. And as an excellent storyteller, she did a good job of making us feel the sadness that weighed heavy in her heart.

"And as sad and disappointing as some of the stories were, she continued to tell them at every grave site and at every cemetery we went to. She told these stories with passion and determination. She made sure the lives and stories of our loved one's would not be forgotten. Every year, every Memorial Day, she told us these stories.

"And eventually, after several hours, we would reach our final destination, which was the last cemetery on our list. And at this last cemetery, she delivered her best storytelling of all.

"All the cemeteries were special, but this last one was probably the most significant, because it was the home of her late husband. His name was Joseph Robinson III. But we knew him as Grandpa Joe. He was a legacy in our family and my grandmother made sure everyone knew his story.

"We heard how he served admirably in the first great war, and how after the war when he returned home, he was

36

falsely accused of a crime. We learned how that accusation resulted in the Klan chasing him and my grandmother from their home down South. How they fled in the middle of the night and had to leave all of their possessions behind.

"We learned how he and my grandmother raised twelve children, how he started his own church and later became a prominent Baptist pastor. We learned how he started his church with just a handful of people who lived on his street, and how that church grew to have over two hundred members.

"We knew all about him. We knew how he lived, and we also knew how he died. He went to heaven while sitting peacefully in his rocking chair. He was a great man. A family man who built my grandmother's house with his bare hands. My grandmother told his story like no one else could.

"He was her hero. He was our hero. From him and her came all of us, and we all understood his importance. Unfortunately, I was a small child when my grandfather died, so I didn't remember him. But I could feel the energy and love that everyone had for him.

"His gravesite was the last stop on our journey, and after this visit we would pack into the cars and head back to my grandmother's house. But before we left, my grandmother would follow one last ritual that she started many, many years ago. Next to Grandpa Joe's grave was a cleared plot of land.

"It was her future resting place. It was kinda weird seeing the place where my grandmother would one day be buried, but we all understood that with life comes death, and we knew that the cleared plot of land was eventually where she would be buried. We all knew that one day she would be buried in that plot of dirt next to my grandfather.

"And just as she did every year, right after she spoke about my grandfather's life, she would glance down at the cleared plot of dirt next to his grave then reach her hand down and gently grab a small sample of dirt. Then she would lift her hand holding the dirt to her lips and gently blow the dirt back to the ground.

"Then she would say 'not today, not today but soon.' Those were the words she quietly murmured. Not today, but soon. She knew that one day that same dirt that she picked up and softly blew back to the ground... she knew one day that dirt would be her eternal ally.

"It would be her eternal neighbor. So, she treated that dirt with a kind of spiritual love and respect. One day that dirt would return the favor and blow back onto her. She knew that would happen, one day it was bound to happen. It just wouldn't be today.

"And then, after that, after watching and hearing her say goodbye to the Earth, we would all head back and pack into the cars to make the trip back to my grandmother's house.

"After being gone for several hours, when we got back to her house, to our delight, all the food was cooked and ready to eat. There were chairs and tables set out for us to sit at. There was good music, playing cards, kickballs, frisbees, and plenty of places to run and play after you finished eating.

"My grandma's house was small, but it had several unique features. It was a three-bedroom house that somehow was big enough for my grandparents to raise twelve children. I always found that to be fascinating.

"At the front of the house was a small porch with two windows on each side. The porch was long and shaded and you could sit out there all day and just relax. There were two rocking chairs on the porch as well as a bunch of plants that hung from above. The plants made the porch look and feel cozy, and also made it appear much larger than it was.

"On the right side of her home was an old storm cellar that led to a large basement area. My grandmother used this space to store homemade jellies, and all different types of fruits and fresh vegetables. She also stored antique furniture, family heirlooms and a bunch of other things down there.

"None of which I found interesting. I never went down in the cellar because it was always cold, dark, and spooky looking. And as someone who was afraid of spiders, that's the last place I ever wanted to enter.

"In the rear of her home and about forty yards away was an old creepy outhouse. It hadn't been used in probably thirty or forty years, and it certainly looked its age. No one, and I can honestly say no one, played near or around that outhouse. It was old and rugged and would probably collapse on the first person who foolishly entered it. Plus, it had spiderwebs in almost every corner that could be seen when you got close to it.

"As kids, we ran around it, but no one dared to enter it. My grandmother said she kept it on her property as a reminder of how things were in the old days. It wasn't much to look at, but it was something that I always remembered.

"To the far left of the outhouse and even further away from the house, was a large chicken coop. And next to the chicken coop was a small pig's pen that housed three to four small pigs and hogs. The pig's pen had the absolute worst smell you could imagine and the closer you got to it the more you wanted to turn around and head in the other direction.

"I remember the pigs and hogs smelled horrible, and just laid around in the mud all day. They laid in the same mud that they pooped and peed in. They were absolutely filthy animals, but we enjoyed watching them.

"Sometimes we even got a chance to feed them. They would eat anything you threw in their direction. They weren't picky eaters. They loved hot dogs, hamburgers, chicken, pizza, cookies and even pie. They ate everything.

"The chickens however were very boring. They didn't do much and they didn't eat much, so there's not much to say about them. The only thing a chicken is good for is eating.

"And finally, on the opposite or other side of my grandmother's house was a large oak tree. It was massive and beautiful, and towered above everything on her property. Everyone loved that oak tree.

"And by everyone, I mean everyone. Not just people, but animals too. There were all types of animals attracted to that tree. There were squirrels, chipmunks, rabbits, racoons, and all types of large birds.

"All of them would stop by to feast on the giant acorns that would continuously drop to the ground. All the animals ate them, but we would pick up these super-sized acorns, and challenge each other to see who could throw them the furthest. That was so much fun.

"And then at the base of the oak tree was a super long dog chain that belonged to Duchess. She was my grandmother's dog. She was an old dog, and much like the chickens, she wasn't very interesting.

"She rarely ever came out of her doghouse. And when she did come out, she would bark and run toward anyone who came close to her. But before she got close to you, she would turn around and run back into her house. And once back inside, she would bark and growl with her nose as the only visible object peering from her doghouse.

"Then after several minutes of barking, she would lie down in her doghouse and drift back to sleep. She was too old to do anything else. My grandmother said Duchess was over twenty years old. Which in dog years would make her something like a hundred or maybe older. My grandmother had that dog since it was a small puppy and over the years, they grew old together.

"There were a lot of memories at my grandmother's house. Duchess, my grandmother, her small house, the hogs, the long dirt road, and the massive oak tree with its super-sized acorns. And of course, there were the never-ending woods that we ran in and out of. Those are the things I remember. The fun times when it was okay to be a kid. When it was okay to run and be wild and explore the inner depths of the woods.

"Those were the times when we created everlasting bonds with our family. I will never forget those days. The days we spent at my grandmother's house. Every year, every Memorial Day, with every member of our family. I will always remember those days.

"And those days would parallel other important times in my family. Over the years we developed bonds that would stick with us forever. And outside of my grandmother's house we created our own family memories.

"There was me, my mother, my father, and my sister April. We had lasting memories too. One such memory was the time when my mother packed us all in the car for a road trip to see one of our aunts. Her name was Aunt Clara."

Chapter 6

The Long Road

After telling the story of my grandmother's house I asked Diana if she was still with me. I knew I had been talking for quite a while, and I asked her if she wanted me to continue. When she nodded and said she did, I continued sharing another memory that had a lasting effect on my family. It was the story of Aunt Clara and a remarkable road trip to see her.

"Aunt Clara was much older than my mother and she lived about six hours away from us in northern Kentucky. Many years ago, after my grandmother passed, my parents moved from Kentucky, which is where most of our family lived, to a small town in Georgia.

"My aunt Clara, seeing herself as a mentor to my mother, would drive down from Kentucky two to three times a year to spend time with us. And every time she came down, she would always bring two of her freshly baked apple pies and her signature dish of apple cinnamon peach cobbler. We absolutely loved Aunt Clara's cooking.

"My mother tried her best, but she could never duplicate Aunt Clara's skills in the kitchen. But on this occasion, Aunt Clara wasn't driving down to see us to bring us tasty pies, we were driving up to see her.

"Her doctor had called my mother and said that our aunt had a large amount of cancer that had spread from her hip all the way up into her spine. The doctor said the cancer spread quickly and had attached itself so deep in Aunt Clara's bones that they couldn't treat it or remove it. He said my aunt's days were numbered, and she was in a great deal of pain.

"She was unable to stand, walk or even move herself in bed. Knowing she didn't have long to live; we all piled in the car and made the six-hour drive to see her. I will always remember that trip my family took to see our Aunt Clara. We were taking a road trip to see her before the cancer claimed her life…

"My father was our driver, and my mother was his eyes and ears on the road. While riding in the passenger seat my mother enjoyed talking to my father and keeping conversations going. She was always talking, and I was always in the back seat listening.

"I remember on that day we had been driving for about three hours, and my father had just mentioned to my mother that we had three more hours to go. My mother then asked him how we were doing on gas.

"My father replied with confidence and said we were good. My father liked challenging the car on long road trips; seeing how far he could drive on a full tank of gas. "He hated stopping for gas unless the tank was almost empty. He believed you got more miles out of a full tank of gas, so he took pride in only filling up right when the gas tank was halfway between the quarter tank line and the empty sign.

"To him that was the best time to fill up. But on this day, he miscalculated. And about an hour later, when my mother asked him how we were doing with gas, my father fidgeted with his response.
"Well, I think we probably need to fill her up… I'm about where I want to be with the gas, but I think we just missed our exit." My mother responded, "Well how far is the next gas exit?"

He replied, "The sign back there said the next gas exit is in twenty miles. I know we can't make it twenty miles. Not where the gas needle is. We need to get off at the next exit and try to find a gas station."

Then my mother chimed in, "Well what sense does that make? If it's not a gas exit, why are we getting off?" My father told her, "We're gonna have to drive down one of those long county roads and see where it leads us. There's bound to be a gas station somewhere. We may have to drive a way to find it, but we'll find one. We don't have a choice. We don't have enough gas to drive twenty miles for the next gas exit."

"So just like that, my father's 'push the gas to the limit challenge' had us exiting off the interstate onto a long county road, and none of us knew where it would take us. The exit we got off on didn't say food, gas, hotels or anything like that. It just said County Road 445. That was it. That was our exit. County Road 445.

"We all hoped we had enough gas in the tank to get us to a gas station. If not, we would be officially stranded in the middle of nowhere. We were all very worried.

"And when we exited the interstate onto the county road, at the end of the off ramp was a stop sign. The only direction we could take was to the right. So that's what we did. We turned right and we just hoped a gas station would be close by.

"Fortunately for us, it was early in the afternoon, and we had plenty of daylight. Had it been dark, our fears would have been magnified, but the lightness of the day made the mood much more positive. When we made our right turn on County Road 445 there was nothing but woods on both sides of the road.

"We drove down that road for what seemed like forever. With nothing but trees and woods on both sides of the road for as far as our eyes could see. We were all worried and hoped and prayed that the car's gas light would not come on.

"And then finally, after driving on this long road for what seemed like an eternity, the woods on both sides of the road sporadically began to open up to farmland. And to our delight, there were now scattered farms on both sides of the road.

"My father's worries of running out of gas began to fade when he joyfully stated, 'where there are farms, there are farmers, and where there are farmers, a gas station is sure to be close by.'

"So, my father kept driving. He drove another mile. Then two and then three. But there was still no gas station in sight. The gas light had still not come on, and he was confident that a gas station would be near. We all sat quietly in the car hoping that his optimism would lead to a fuel reward.

"We were all hopeful but deep inside we were all very worried. All we could do was sit quietly in our seats and silently pray for a gas station to appear. Then, out of nowhere, the quietness inside the car was interrupted.

"My mother had suddenly become worried and paranoid. But it wasn't because of our gas situation. It was something else that bothered her. And when she frantically raised her voice and asked my father a strange question it made us all uneasy.

"By now my mother had all but turned her head and shoulders around toward her passenger side window and was focused on something that we had just driven past. She saw something on the side of the road that startled her. Something that had alarmed her, and eventually alarmed us as well.

"Oh my God Darryl, did you see that?" my mother frantically blurted out.

My father, who was totally focused on nothing but the car's gas needle responded, "See what babe? What was I supposed to see?"

"Oh God Darryl. That house back there! How did you not see it? We have to turn around! We have to! Something's not right."

"At this point I didn't know what was going on, and neither did my sister or my father. No one saw what my mother saw, but we all were puzzled at what she could have seen that alarmed her like it did.

"She was worried, and her face showed it. My father, out of compliance, immediately pulled off to the side of the road and made a U-turn. On most any other occasion he would never have turned around, especially with the car being so low on fuel.

"But on this day, he did so without hesitation. And when my father turned around, he didn't have to drive very far before he saw what had frightened and worried my mother. My mother frantically pointed to a house on the side of the road and told my father to pull into its driveway.

"When my father pulled into the driveway he stared at the house and had the same look of worry on his face as my mother did. For a few long seconds it was quiet inside our car. Everyone was silent and everyone was shocked.

"The silence was broken when my mother looked at my father and asked him a question. She said, "Darryl, do you see this? This is crazy!" My father slowly nodded and shook his head in agreement. And then he said, "This house looks awfully familiar. Something is definitely not right here. This is just not right."

46

"The house that had startled my parents was a mysterious house that looked a lot like my grandmother's house. But her house was three hours away in Kentucky, and we were somewhere in Georgia on County Road 445. None of this made any sense.

"The home we pulled up to was abandoned and neglected, but it was eerily similar to my grandmother's. From the driveway we could clearly see the front of the house. It was almost an exact replica of the front of my grandmother's home. It had a small porch, with two windows on each side. Just as my grandmother's porch had.

"At this point we were all extremely puzzled. And as we all silently stared at the house, my father began to slowly pull further up the driveway. And then when he came to a stop, things got even stranger.

"Just ahead of us on the right side of the house was a storm cellar. It looked exactly like the one on the side of my grandmother's house. The one where she stored her fruits and jellies and antique furniture. We couldn't believe what we were seeing.

"And then when we looked straight in front of us, thirty or so yards ahead, there it was... the old outhouse. It looked eerily similar to the abandoned outhouse on my grandmother's property. The one she had refused to tear down.

"We were all amazed. We were all speechless. Our hearts were pounding with fear. But my father didn't hit reverse and turn around. He continued to slowly pull further ahead along the driveway. And when he pulled all the way to its end, we were even more alarmed and confused with what we saw.

"To the far left and a few yards from the rear of the home was an abandoned chicken coop. The same chicken coop that was home to the uninteresting chickens at my

47

grandmother's house. We couldn't believe what we were seeing.

"At this point my father had seen enough, and immediately put the car in reverse and pulled off the property. As we pulled out of the driveway, we all looked at the house in complete disbelief. I loved going to my grandmother's house and I remembered everything about it, and this house appeared to be exactly the same as my grandmother's house.

"But how could this be? My grandmother lived several hours from where we were. This was strange and scary to say the least. As we slowly drove away from the house our eyes shifted to the other side of the home. And to no one's surprise, on the opposite side was a large oak tree.

"It was a massive tree, and from my view I could see tons of giant-sized acorns on the ground beneath it. And at the base of the tree was a long-abandoned dog chain. There was no dog or doghouse, just a long chain. A long, rusted chain like the one used to chain Duchess.

"Everyone in the car was speechless. We couldn't believe what we had just seen. It was impossible. There was no way for that house to look like it did. There was no way for that house to be a carbon copy of my grandmother's home.

"My grandfather built my grandmother's home with his bare hands. And he built it at least three hours from where we were. None of this made any sense.

"As my father headed back down the long county road, the car was once again silent. My mother, who always welcomed conversation, was as quiet as the rest of us.

"I could hear her and my father whispering to each other about how none of this made any sense. My mother was a very religious woman who prayed tirelessly, but she didn't pray on this occasion. She was so worried and confused that all she could do was shake her head in disbelief.

"Nothing could explain how, or why that house was an exact replica of my grandmother's house. The conversations between my mother and my father eventually were no longer whispers and began to increase in volume. Their voices gradually picked up to a point that included my sister and I in their conversation.

"They asked me for my thoughts, but the only thing I could say was that I thought it was strange. I told my parents that I remembered grandma's house and at first, I thought that house was her house. I told my mom I knew it wasn't my grandma's house because I didn't see the long dirt road.

"As a 13-year-old kid that's what I was focused on. I was more focused on what I didn't see. And I didn't see the long dirt road. That's all I said, and they didn't ask me anything else.

"My sister, who was much older than me, couldn't rationalize what had just happened either. When they asked her to chime in, all she could say was she didn't know. She just said she couldn't explain it.

"At this point we were still driving and nearing the end of the long county road. At the end of the road my father reached a stop sign and had an option to go left or right. Both options looked the same. Another long county road awaited us either way we turned. And this new road we were turning on was County Road 448.

"When my father asked us which way we should go, for some strange reason we all said to go right. I don't know why we all chose that direction, but our hunch paid off when about a mile up the road a small gas station appeared.

"It was old and neglected and only had one working gas pump. But it was open, and it had gas, and that's all that mattered to us. When my father pulled into the gas station a

49

man from inside walked out and met him at the pump. He told my father he would pump the gas for him.

"This old gas station offered full service. That meant they would pump your gas, check your tire pressure, and clean your front and rear windshields while you waited in your car. As the man pumped the gas, my father rolled down his window and asked him about County Road 445.

"He asked the man if he was familiar with it, and the man said he didn't know much about it other than you have to take that road to get to the interstate. He said everybody drives on that road, but that he didn't know much more than that. He asked my father why he asked about the road and if we were lost.

"My father told him that we weren't lost but that we saw a house on that road that strongly resembled the house of a family member. A family member who lived many miles and many hours away. He told the man that the house had startled us, and that he was curious who owned the property.

"The man said he didn't know anything about the house but offered a suggestion that my father welcomed. He told my father that when he went back down that road to write down the address and look it up when we got wherever we were going. This suggestion made a lot of sense, and everyone in the car shook their heads in agreement.

"So, when we headed back toward County Road 445, my mother took out an ink pen and prepared to write down the home's address. As my father turned back onto the road he drove very slowly. As he drove slowly past the scattered farm homes, we all anxiously awaited the chance to lay our eyes on the mysterious home once more.

"All of our heads and eyes were aimed at the homes on the left side of the road. My mother had her notepad and pen and was ready to write down the address. My father

50

continued to drive slowly and crept along the long county road for what seemed like an eternity. At some point, the farmhouses gave way to woods on both sides of the street, and we realized we had missed the house.

"My father had surprisingly driven all the way to the end of the road and somehow, we missed the mysterious house. The only thing we saw was the sign at the end of the road to get back onto the interstate. Somehow my father had driven past it, somehow, we all missed it.

"So, with a full tank of gas, my father turned the car around and he headed back down the county road again. He was determined not to miss the house this time. 'We must have driven by it. I must have been driving too fast.' That's all he kept saying.

"He told everyone to keep their eyes open as he made the U-turn on the road. He drove slowly. Even more slowly than the last time. But once again, we found ourselves at the end of the long road, and somehow, we had missed the house again. After making two trips and driving several miles to both ends of the long county road, we missed the house yet again.

"We were all extremely puzzled. As hard and focused as we were on spotting the house, somehow, we missed it for a second time. My father had reached the stop sign. The same one which we all decided to turn right at. The same one that was a mile from the gas station.

"He had now driven down this long road three times. The first time revealed the home but the last two times it seemed to escape us. So, on this last drive my father made another U-turn and headed back down the road again. For the *fourth* time.

"This time he drove extra slowly. Even slower than the last time if that was at all possible. And much slower than the time before that. He wanted to be sure we didn't drive

51

past the house. He wanted to be sure my mother would be able to write down the address. But just like our efforts on our second and third trips looking for the house, we were unsuccessful.

"As my father reached the end of the road the interstate sign appeared again. And this time he proceeded ahead and drove onto the interstate. As we exited County Road 445, we all had chills. The strange house that had startled us had mysteriously disappeared. It vanished. It was gone.

"No one could explain what we had just witnessed, so for the remaining trip to see Aunt Clara, nobody mentioned it again. It shocked and scared us all. It was such a disturbing moment, that as a family we never spoke about it again. In our minds, we couldn't explain it, so we silently agreed to never discuss it. And that was one of the memories and moments that my family created. A memory and moment so powerful and inexplicable that we silently agreed to never discuss or mention it again."

Diana was amazed when I finished telling my story. She said, "Oh my God. That was an amazing story. I have chills all up and down my arms. That was definitely mysterious. I've never experienced anything like that. The way you tell the story is so natural. I could have almost pictured myself in the car with y'all. I could feel the suspense.

"I have always believed that there are things that can't be explained. And that would definitely be one of them. I also believe we all have the ability to tap into our spiritual side. We all have a way to project and absorb energy. Think of it this way… we can say more about how we feel through our body language than actual words. Do you believe we can communicate with each other through our thoughts?"

I said, "Yeah, I do. I don't know how that works but it sounds about right. I know facial expressions say a lot about our emotions. Is that what you mean?"

She replied, "Not really. I'm talking about something deeper than that. If it's okay with you, can I show you?"

"Sure," I said, "have at it."

Diana said, "Okay. So, let's try this. Place both your hands flat on the table and follow my lead. I want you to look at me and try to feel what I'm telling you. Try to feel my energy. I'm not gonna say anything. I'm just gonna look into your eyes."

I placed both my hands flat on the table as she told me to and at first it seemed odd to be doing this in Starbucks. I was sure people around us were watching and wondering what we were doing. But I blocked them out, and I was completely focused on her.

At first, I couldn't feel anything, and as I looked into her eyes, I wasn't sure what I was doing. It felt kinda weird with me staring at her, and her staring back at me. The only thing I could feel was the cold table underneath my hands.

Then everything suddenly changed when Diana took both her hands and placed them atop mine. She was quiet, still, and focused. And then her straight and focused face turned to a somewhat half smile. It was as if she was inviting me in. Inviting me into her mind. And as she smiled at me, I felt the gates to her thoughts open.

At that exact moment, while I was sitting at the table and staring into her eyes, I began to feel her energy. As I looked into her eyes, I could feel a small, cool breeze gently brush across my face. I don't know where it came from, but it was real.

I felt like I was feeling her soul. I felt the loneliness she had when her mother died. I felt the love she had for her son. I could feel her likes and dislikes.

53

Sitting at that table, sitting across from her, I felt a ton of emotions. They were strange, powerful emotions that gave me the chills. She had opened up to me and I could feel everything.

I couldn't explain what I was feeling, but it was natural and calming. It almost felt as if we were alone in that Starbucks. I had officially zoned out and I was only seeing and feeling her.

And then, after what felt like forever, but in actuality was only about thirty seconds, Diana removed her hands from atop of mine and asked me a question.
She said, "So Curtis, what did you feel?"

I said, "I felt everything, and it was a beautiful and powerful feeling. I felt a gentle breeze move across my face and it gave me chills. I think I felt your spirit. When you placed your hands on top of mine, I could feel your heart. I felt it beating. It was an amazing experience. It was calm, cool, and inviting."

She said, "Well that's good. I'm glad you felt that. But what was I telling you? What message did my energy give you?"

"I'm not sure," I answered her honestly, "I've never done that before. I've never felt anything like that in my life. But I felt like you were inviting me in. Like you wanted me to be a part of you. A part of your life.

"Kinda like… your soulmate. I felt like… well, I felt like… like you love me. I felt loved. I felt loved by you. I know we haven't known each other long, but I felt like you kinda were telling me you loved me. I know that sounds weird, and I'm sorry to say that but that's what I felt."

And when I said that, Diana didn't respond. She just listened. She had a somewhat straight face and seemed caught off guard by my response. Clearly my answer was not what she expected, because she quickly changed the subject.

54

She asked me where I put the paper that she wrote her email address on and reminded me to send her a copy of one of my stories. After that she started packing her things. Our meeting and conversation were over.

She said, "Well it's about time for me to go. I have to pick up my son and if I'm late they're gonna charge me. And I don't want that. But hey, I really enjoyed spending time with you. It's nice to be in the company of such an intelligent and handsome gentleman."
Then she smiled at me and said the words I was really hoping to hear.

"So, I'm making a schedule change for tomorrow. Let's meet here again. Same time and hopefully the same seats? We have to discuss this story you're gonna send me. I can't wait to read it."

Then Diana stood up from the table and prepared to leave. But before she left, she leaned toward me and gave me a warm hug. As we hugged, she took both her hands and rubbed the back of my shoulders and whispered "thank you" in my ear. And then she left.

As I watched her walk away, I could not believe what just happened. In only two days I had made a connection with what seemed to be the woman of my dreams. I just couldn't believe it. I felt like I was in love.

I know some people don't believe you can have love at first sight, but I believed I found it. The chemistry was there, and everything lined up perfectly. Diana appeared to be everything I could ask for. And we had another date set for tomorrow. Another opportunity for me to be in her presence. I couldn't believe how all of this was falling into place.

As soon as I got home, I searched my computer to find a copy of the story I promised to send her. This would be her first chance to read my work and I wanted to make sure it was ready. Ready for her opinion. Ready for her feedback.

And even though I had written it several years ago, it was what I considered my best work. It was the most meaningful piece of literature I had ever written. I knew I needed to read over it for errors.

I wanted to be sure it checked all the boxes. So, I opened my saved documents and hit the search tab. And when I found it, I went right to work reading it. I read the whole story line by line. It was titled *The Older Boys* and it began with an introduction to my life growing up as a teen.

Chapter 7

Black Birds

In my house there was me, my mom, my dad, and my sister. My sister's name was April, and she was seven years older than me. And even though she was older than me we got along very well. Everyone in our family got along well.

My parents rarely ever argued, and my sister and I both were well taken care of. My mother was the matriarch of our family. She was a strong and firm woman who made sure my sister and I knew the importance of doing the right thing. She made sure we stayed on top of our grades at school and raised us to be respectable people at home and in the community.

My father was a hardworking man who worked two jobs, and a ton of hours so we could have the things we needed. But for all the hours he worked and money he made, he rarely ever spent any of it on himself. So, when my mother encouraged him to buy a new car, one just for him, he was thrilled.

With my mother's blessing he bought a really nice blue sports car that he absolutely cherished. On his days off from work he washed it and vacuumed it and made sure it smelled just as good as it looked. And on those rare days when he was off work from both his jobs, my father would pile us all in the car and we would enjoy long rides through the country.

We all loved riding in my father's car. Especially when he would let all the windows down so we could feel the cool breeze blowing against our faces. It was a wonderful feeling. One we all loved. Then one day tragedy struck our home, and all those fun and memorable rides came to an end.

On that fateful day, my father was driving alone down a long county road not far from our home. In front of his car on the right shoulder of the road was a large flock of black buzzards. By all accounts there were anywhere from three to five birds, who were all feasting on a large roadkill. I don't know if it was a dead dog or a cat, or a possum or an armadillo, but whatever it was it had their full attention.

As my father's vehicle approached, all the birds began to attack each other by aggressively flapping their wings and hopping up and down. They were fighting and jockeying not to lose position over the kill. And just as my father's car passed the birds, one unlucky bird flapped its wings upwards and then backwards and was pulled into the passenger side window of my father's car.

My father, who was notorious for riding with his windows down, panicked when the bird landed in his passenger seat and immediately swerved hard to the left. Unfortunately, when he swerved left, he swerved right into the path of an approaching truck. The collision between the two vehicles instantly killed my father, the driver of the truck and the large buzzard.

To make matters worse, just before the accident, the bird had somehow landed in my father's lap, and when the vehicles collided, the bird's beak and its entire head were embedded in my father's throat. It was a terrible accident, and the people who witnessed my fathers mutilated body were forever shaken.

The large black bird's head had to be cut at the neck to be released from my father's throat. It was a tragic end to a good man's life. My family was devastated. My father didn't deserve to go out like that.

And after his death, my mother was left to care for me and my sister. And even though my sister was already grown when my father died, we were all traumatized and needed the care and support that only my mother could provide. And as weak and broken as she was, she found the strength to pull us back together.

She told us we had to keep living. She made sure we didn't let our father's death keep us from living our lives and reaching our full potential. So, we eventually moved on.

We moved on with our lives because we had to. It was a sad chapter in my life where I learned the true meaning of a tragedy. And throughout my life I would witness a few more tragedies. Some of them I wrote about and others I just locked in the back of my head as memories.

After the death of my father, we were officially on our own. Me, my mother, and my sister April. It was just the three of us. We had plenty of family to lean on but for the most part we relied on each other. This was a difficult time for us, but fortunately for me I had several friends in my neighborhood that I came to rely on.

They took my mind off me missing my father. They were like my brothers. We had known each other since elementary school. So, in my mind they weren't *like* my brothers, they *were* my brothers.

Chapter 8

Train Tracks

First there was Tim. He was a tall, skinny kid that liked to climb trees and build forts in the woods. He absolutely loved being outside. Staying in the house and playing video games was not his thing. He was an outdoorsman.

Tim had planned to go into the military after high school, and I knew he would make a great soldier. Whenever I went outside to play, the first door I knocked on was his. He was sure to find something fun for us to do.

Next there was Joe. He was the athlete of the group. He played basketball, football and also ran track. He wasn't just good, he was the star player on every team he played on. And even though he was only in ninth grade, he was the starting running back for our high school football team.

He spent most of his afternoons at football practice, but when he got home, he would find us and join in with whatever we were doing. And he was cool. If any of us ever had a problem with someone at school, Joe was always there to make sure it didn't escalate.

Being friends with him had a lot of benefits. He was popular, and because he hung out with us, we were popular too. And like me, Joe also only had one parent. His mother was a single parent who raised him and his two older brothers alone.

But unlike me, Joe never met his father, and his upbringing was very different from mine. My parents were very strict, and we had rules and chores that we had to do. But Joe's house was different.

Joe's mom worked nights and he and his brothers only saw her on the weekends. When they got home from school, she was at work, and they practically raised themselves. And that's not always a good thing.

Joe's oldest brother's name was Wayne. He got in a lot of trouble over the years and spent some time in jail. He actually spent several years in jail. He was cool and real street savvy. He was always teaching Joe about the streets and how to protect himself.

His other brother's name was Mark. And just like Wayne, he got into trouble too. When he was in high school, he was the star quarterback, and had all kinds of scholarship offers to some really big-time schools. But colleges backed away when he got caught selling marijuana at school and got kicked off the team.

He eventually dropped out of school. He was not as outgoing as his brothers, and he mostly stuck to himself. He would walk around the neighborhood by himself and just pace up and down the street. He didn't do much. He worked odd jobs, rode the city bus to work and kept to himself.

Those were Joe's brothers, and unfortunately, they were his role models.
But Joe vowed to not follow down the same path as them. He was a good student, and he had a mentor from some men's group that checked in on him from time to time to keep him straight.

Joe was doing things the right way. He was on the right path. Everyone was rooting for him, and we knew he was gonna make it big.

And then there was Larry. He was a fat kid that hung out with us. And he was a really cool kid. He never let his weight get in the way of having a good time. At school he got a lot of fat jokes from other kids. But they didn't bother him like they would other kids, he actually welcomed them in a way.

If a kid laughed at him and called him fat, Larry would crack back and talk about that kid's clothes or shoes, or whatever else they had on that stood out. He had a way of cracking back when people tried to talk about him. He was quick on his feet and would crack back and make the other kids back off.

He was funny, confident and a lot of people liked him. I remember one time during lunch, when an older kid came to our table and started telling jokes about Larry's weight, and the food he was eating, Larry had two big slices of pizza and a diet coke on his tray.

When the older kid started cracking on Larry everybody started laughing. And then Larry started cracking back and the back and forth between them was hilarious. Larry talked about the zits on the kids face, and then he talked about the tight pants the guy had on. And then Larry talked about how the guy had little hands.

It was crazy. They went back and forth on each other, and they had everybody laughing. That's how Larry was. He was always ready if someone came after him with fat people jokes. He was definitely fat, and he was also super cool.

But Larry's weight was an issue. He had a lot of health problems because of his weight. He ate a lot of the wrong things and because of that he had high blood pressure, breathing problems and a couple other things. He knew he was fat, and he knew he needed to lose a few pounds, but he never did.

He just didn't let his weight stop him from being a kid. He was big and fat and funny, and we all enjoyed being around him. We accepted him for who he was, and we were all good friends.

So that was my crew. Me, Tim, Larry, and Joe. We called ourselves the four amigos. We were always around each other. At school and at home. And my mother was okay with my friends.

She had one rule for me and that was for me to make sure I was home before dark. As long as I did that, she let me hang with the boys whenever I wanted to. We were always together.

And we weren't mischievous kids either. We didn't get into trouble, and we weren't looking for any trouble to get into. Most times when we hung out, we just walked the train tracks and played in the woods behind our homes.

The woods behind our homes must have stretched for about a hundred yards and then they opened up to the train tracks. And on the other side of the train tracks were more woods. We didn't know how far those woods on the other side of the tracks went, but there were times when we went way deep into the woods.

And when we played in those woods, we had a ball. We built all kinds of forts, above ground and underground. We climbed trees, pretended we were soldiers, built traps to catch rabbits and squirrels and sometimes we just walked for miles and miles along the tracks.

I also remember we walked for what seemed like days in those woods. At first, when we went deep into the woods, we had to use sticks and markers to help us find our way back. But after a while we got so comfortable in the woods that we didn't need any markers. We knew where we were. We knew how to navigate around the trees and brush.

We knew what trees to look for and what paths to take. We knew those woods like the back of our hands. We got so good at getting around in those woods that we nicknamed ourselves the woodsmen.

One day while we were deep in the woods we stumbled on a creek. It was cool finding that, but we couldn't play in it or explore it after we noticed a large water moccasin laying on its bank. Those snakes were dangerous and extremely poisonous, so we dared not play in the creek or attempt to cross it.

The last thing we wanted was for one of us to get bit by a snake, so we just explored the woods on our side of the creek. That was our cutoff line. Not being able to go to the other side of the creek was disappointing but there were plenty of woods to explore on our side.

I remember one time we brought a shovel with us and used it to build an underground fort. We started digging this massive hole in the ground and then we covered it with pieces of plywood we got from a dumpster. We carved out holes in the dirt walls with our hands and then later used those slots to put candles in.

When we lit the candles in our underground fort, it was super cool. We thought that the fort would last forever. Then one day it rained really hard for like two days and the next day when we went out to check on it, the weight of the rain and wet dirt had caused the roof to cave in. So that was the end of that fort, but we built several more just like it.

And if we weren't building forts or exploring the woods, we were pretending we were soldiers. We would act like we were looking for the enemy and quietly move and hide through the woods. We had homemade bows and arrows and spears and sharp sticks.

We would fill our pockets with large rocks and stones. We had all kinds of weapons. We even had portable radios we used to communicate and find each other in the woods.

We had a great time in those woods. And when we weren't playing in the woods, we had even more fun walking along the train tracks. Sometimes we saw Joe's brothers walking with several other guys along the tracks. But before they could see us, we would hide in the woods and secretly watch them as they passed by.

Most times they walked right by us and didn't even know we were hiding there watching them. And as we hid in the woods, Tim would whisper "As soldiers, we have to be very quiet. We can never be seen or heard."

We would spy on them all the time. It would be three, four and sometimes even five of those guys just walking the train track and hanging out. They were much older than us and most times we saw them they were either drinking beers or smoking marijuana.

A few other times they had girls with them. And even though two of them were Joe's brothers we always stayed out of their way. They were much older than us, so we came up with a name for them. We called them 'The Older Boys.'

While the older boys were walking the tracks and probably reminiscing about what their lives might have been, when *we* walked the track, we talked about our futures. We talked about what we were going to be after high school. Mark knew he was going to the pros, so he talked about playing for the Dallas Cowboys.

He talked about how he was gonna be a first-round draft pick. He bragged about having over thirty football scholarship offers and said he wanted to go to the University of Georgia. And that's all he talked about… going to play football at Georgia and then the Dallas Cowboys.

Tim wanted to be a soldier. He said he was going to the military as soon as he graduated. He wanted to be a Marine and made sure everybody knew it.

This guy would get down and do push-ups on the train tracks. Other times he would camouflage himself by lying in the dirt and covering himself with leaves. He would

65

walk around with no shirt on while he carried a long Rambo-like knife.

He was always focused on being a soldier. When we asked him what job he was gonna have in the military he said he wanted to be a sniper. We all laughed cause it was funny but deep down we knew he was serious. Tim was a diehard soldier.

And Larry, well he said he wanted to be a comedian. He was always cracking jokes on people and making folks laugh. And even though he was fat, he was confident with himself.

While walking down the train tracks Larry would call out all the heavy-set comedians and talk about how being fat didn't stop them. He told us his stage name was gonna be Fat Larry and said as soon as he turned eighteen, he was going to try his luck in a comedy club. He said he didn't care if the people were white, black or even aliens. He said he knew he could make anybody laugh.

As for me, I didn't know what I wanted to do. My mother had plans for me to go to college and be something special, but I wasn't thinking about anything back then. I was just happy to be out of the house with my friends.

All I thought about was my friends. Careers and jobs and things like that didn't interest me. I was only interested in having fun.

But one day those fun days on the tracks would take a turn. Something different was about to happen. Something much more noteworthy and adventurous than anything we had ever done. It was a day I will never forget.

That day started when I got off the school bus after a short ride home from school. After I walked into my house, I put my bookbag down on the kitchen counter, poured a glass of water, guzzled it down and then went right back out the door to have fun with my friends. When I went outside the first thing, I did was walk down the street to Larry's house.

He lived a few houses down from me. When he looked out the window and saw me walking toward his house, he opened his front door and yelled to me he would be right out. As I waited in his driveway, I could see Joe from a distance down the road.

I yelled his name, and he started walking toward me. Since Joe wasn't on the bus today, I didn't think he went to school. I was calling him over to see what he had been doing all day. And by the time he got halfway down the street Tim looked out the window and saw Joe walking toward me, so he came outside too.

Before I knew it the three of us were standing outside Larry's house waiting for him to come out. Just like that, we were all together and ready to have some fun. When Larry finally came out, he said he wanted to walk along the train tracks and have a rock throwing contest.

When I said I was cool with-it Tim and Joe both said they were cool with it too. So, we headed toward the woods behind our homes to begin our afternoon of fun. While walking, I asked Joe why he didn't ride the bus today and if he went to school.

He said he didn't go to school but went up there after school to lift weights with a few of his teammates. But when only a few of them showed up he called his brother to come get him. He said he was hoping we had something cool planned because he had been in the house all day doing nothing. He said he was ready to get out of the house and hang with us.

Once we cut through the woods, we reached the train tracks in no time. Then we started stuffing our pockets with large and heavy rocks to throw. Once we all had our best rocks, Larry started things off and our rock throwing contests began.

First, we competed to see who could throw the rocks the furthest. Then we competed to see who could throw them the highest. And after that we set up a few targets and tested our accuracy.

Then when we finished our rock throwing competition it was time to walk the tracks and see who could skip their rocks along the narrow edges of the tracks. That was the coolest task and required the most skill. None of us were good at that but we all tried our best.

Chapter 9

A Dog Gone Problem

And then as we walked along the tracks tossing our rocks, a medium-sized, hairy yellow dog appeared out of nowhere. He came from out of the woods. The dog initially just sat off to the side and watched us as we threw the rocks.

From what I could see the dog appeared to be pregnant. It had long nipples that touched the ground as it walked. And when Tim whistled for the dog, she came right to him.

And when the dog got close, we could see that she was a very friendly, well fed yellow lab. She was a smart dog. As Tim patted her, she wagged her tail and licked his hand. Then Tim gave her a gentle pat on the head and motioned her to go away.

She was a really smart dog and started walking back toward the woods as Tim had instructed her. We wondered where the dog came from and if it had somehow gotten lost. But we all agreed that she seemed okay, so we ignored it and continued walking the tracks and throwing our rocks.

The dog seemed interested with what we were doing so she stayed close behind and tagged along. She must have walked with us for about forty or fifty yards when all the sudden she turned around and started walking back toward the wooded area from where she appeared. We all watched the dog and wondered what it was up to.

Then when she seemingly looked at Tim and started to bark, we knew this was a smart dog. We knew that bark met something. The dog was trying to get Tim's attention. It walked into the edge of the woods and waited to see if Tim would follow.

And when he didn't follow her, she reappeared from the woods and started to bark again. At this point we all knew the dog wanted Tim's attention. The dog clearly wanted Tim to follow it.

Tim said, "She must have a bunch of puppies in there. Maybe one of them is injured or something. Maybe she needs help getting them across the tracks?"

We didn't know what was going on, but we all agreed to follow the dog. Once we got close to the area where the dog was, she shot in front of us straight into the woods. The dog stayed about twenty yards in front of us, and constantly looked back to see if we were following. If we stopped walking, she would stop leading us.

And when we acted like we were gonna turn around she would start to bark. This was definitely a smart dog. Way smarter than any dog we'd ever been around. By my account we must have followed that dog for every bit of five to maybe ten minutes.

We were following that dog for quite a while. And because we knew the area well, we knew that we still weren't that far from the tracks. And as we followed the dog, we were all curious and anxious to see where the dog was taking us to.

Then, after several more minutes, we realized we were coming up on the creek, which was pretty deep in the woods. We knew we had a decision to make. We were officially deep in the woods.

Then Tim said, "If that dog doesn't lead us to something soon, we probably need to turn around." Mark agreed with him saying, "I bet she's taking us to a litter of puppies. And watch all of them be dead." Then Larry tried to add a little humor when he said, "Well if the puppies are dead, we can always create our very own pet cemetery back here. And when we go to sleep at night, we're gonna have a bunch of crazy, possessed newborn puppies standing over our beds, staring and licking their baby chops at us."

We all laughed at Larry's joke. That humor was needed and seemed to break the tension that was clearly growing thicker by the minute. And then, all of the sudden the dog stopped. And when she stopped, she started to whine, and within minutes her puppies started to appear from the brush.

One by one they appeared from the surrounding woods. First, we counted one, then two, then three, then four. Then two more puppies popped up. There was a total of six puppies that had appeared from the brush.

And when they appeared, one by one they went right to their mother who welcomed them. We all celebrated when we saw the mother and her puppies together. It was an amazing site to see the puppies reconnected with their mother. But as we cheered and celebrated, Tim was much more skeptical. He was much more cautious.

He immediately became very suspicious when he saw all the puppies. He said, "Have you noticed how big these puppies are? They aint no newborns. And have you noticed that none of her puppies came over to suckle her nipples? Her pups are much older. She's not breast feeding those dogs. They eat real food. Somethings wrong with this picture."

We didn't think anything of what he said. We all thought Tim was just acting paranoid. So, we turned back and started walking back toward the tracks. But when we turned around and started to walk back to the tracks the dog started to bark again.

This time her bark was much, much louder. Much more aggressive. When we turned around to see what the dog was up to, we saw her running way ahead of her puppies.

She ran all the way to the edge of the creek, then turned back and started barking again. Then she barked several more times, then ran across the creek and waited for us to follow. We knew what that dogs bark met. She was trying to tell us something.

She wanted us to follow her again. We knew she had already proven to be a smart dog by leading us to her puppies. But Tim had a different analysis of what was happening. He said, "See, I told y'all. She didn't bring us all the way out here for those pups. She left them behind.

And now she ran all the way across the creek. And that thing is full of snakes. She wants us to keep following her. She tryna tell us something. What do y'all think we should do?"

Everyone but Larry agreed to keep following the dog. We had come this far and wanted to see what the dog was up to. Seeing those puppies was crazy, and now we were curious what lay ahead.

But Larry wasn't feeling it. He said, "We been deep in these woods a million times, but we never crossed that creek. For one, it has snakes in it. And two, we don't know what's over there on the other side.

We aint never crossed that creek and now y'all gonna follow a stray dog over there? Y'all are crazy. All of y'all. But if y'all wanna go y'all can go. But I'm staying right here."

One by one we told him we were going, and if he wasn't comfortable going, he could wait there with the puppies. Which is what he did. So, Larry found a tree, leaned against it and said, "I'll be waiting right here when y'all get back."

Then Tim said, "Well if we're not back in fifteen minutes are you gonna come looking for us?" We all laughed. And then Larry said, "If y'all aint back in fifteen minutes, I'm hauling ass outta here." We all laughed again.

And then we kept going. We crossed that mystical creek and followed the yellow dog. To our surprise the creek wasn't as scary as we thought. We didn't see any snakes, and the creek was surprisingly very shallow.

As we followed the dog, she constantly kept looking back to see if we were following her. She was determined to lead us to something, and we were determined to follow her. We didn't have to follow the dog for long, because after three or four minutes she suddenly stopped.

She stopped in her tracks, sat on the ground, and started to whine. And once again we knew what that meant. As we slowly approached the dog, we knew she had brought us to whatever it was that she wanted us to see. As we walked up to the dog, Tim kneeled down and patted the dog on the head and said, "Now what is it you brought us out here for? What are you tryna tell us girl?"

When we looked around, at first, we didn't see anything. But when Tim looked, he saw something we didn't. He pointed out a small opening in the middle of the woods about fifty yards in front of us. Just beyond the thick brush was a small path or clearing of sorts.

As we walked closer, we could see that the clearing appeared to be man-made. It was strange and appeared out of nowhere. We were in the middle of the woods and directly in front of us was some sort of clearing or path. As we got closer, we saw several low hanging tree branches that had been cut, and the brush leading to the opening lay flatly pressed against the ground. It was clear someone or something had walked along this path.

By now we were all nervous, worried, and afraid. Our slow casual walk through the woods had turned into something much more careful. By now we were tiptoeing and walking as cautiously and quietly as we could.

We didn't know what lay ahead and we needed to be stealthy. All of the games we played in the woods were nothing compared to this. This was the real deal. When we got to the clearing and looked directly ahead of us, our predictions were right.

The clearing was definitely man made. And directly in the middle of the clearing was a small tent. A tent in the middle of the woods, in the middle of nowhere. We didn't know what to think or what to do. None of this made any sense.

Chapter 10

Costly Decisions

As we were all hunched down, we all quietly stared at the tent and wondered what to make of it. Joe whispered, "It's just so out of place. Why is it here? There's nothing out here." Then Tim chimed in and said, "Since when is it a crime to have a tent in the woods. That's what they make them for. So you can hide out and live in the woods. People do it all the time. I've slept in a tent before."

Then Joe said, "Well I get that, but why did that dog lead us all the way out here? She clearly wanted us to follow her. And that's a smart dog. Something must be wrong. One of us needs to go and take a look inside the tent. We gotta see what's in there."

Then I said, "Well, I think you should go Tim. You like stuff like this. Plus, you know more about tents than the rest of us." Then Joe and Tim had a brief conversation between the two of them.

Joe said, "Yeah Tim, go ahead and take a look bro."

"Since when do y'all get to decide and tell me what to do?" said Tim.

To which Joe responded, "Well somebody's gotta check it out. And you were the main one telling us to follow the dog out here. So yeah, I think you should go."

Then Tim said, "Well Ima go, but y'all better get my back if something jumps off."

And Joe and I chorused, "We got you bro. Now hurry up and get over there. Go take a look."

At that point Tim left our side and cautiously walked toward the tent. He walked very softly and tried hard not to crackle leaves under his feet. Though he loved the woods and was a soldier at heart, I could tell he was scared.

We all were. And as Joe and I sat hunched down in the brush, all we could do was watch Tim. Each step he took seemed like an eternity. My heart was pounding, and I wanted this to be over. But I knew Tim had to look inside that tent.

The dog we followed here was laying on the ground next to us. Neither the dog nor Joe or I made a sound. Our eyes were on Tim who continued to creep toward the tent.

There was stillness in the air. Everything seemed to stop. Everything but my heart which was pounding and beating from inside my chest. I was nervous and afraid that something might go wrong. The tension in the air was thick.

As we watched Tim creep closer and closer, I wondered why anyone in their right mind would place a tent so far back in the woods. There was absolutely nothing out here. Then I wondered why the dog had led us out here.

As Tim approached the tent my mind was racing with all sorts of thoughts. Joe and I both watched in awe as Tim put aside his fears and walked steadily toward the tent. Neither one of us said a word, but I'm sure he was thinking the same thoughts I was.

Joe might have been tougher than me, but I knew he was just as afraid as I was. You could hear a pin drop as we watched Tim get near and then peek his head inside the tent. Then the quietness and silence were broken when Tim immediately pulled his head from the tent and turned and ran back toward us.

He was running fast and as he got closer, I could see fear all over his face. It was like he had seen a ghost. Tim was definitely startled. Something in that tent had terrified him. Without saying a word, Joe and I both knew something was wrong.

On his way to the tent Tim tiptoed and tried not to make a sound. But on his run back he stepped on any and every leaf and branch in his path.

My heart was racing. I was almost terrified to ask Tim what he saw in that tent. And when he approached us, I didn't have to ask him any questions. Tim immediately began speaking in a hurried and worried tone.

As he spoke, he was so upset that he could barely catch his breath. He was talking fast and whispering as he spoke. He said, "Guys, you won't believe this. There's a kid in there. Like four, maybe four or five years old. A white kid. And he's asleep.

And he's naked. He's skinny. And he's lying in there on his side curled up. Oh my God. He was naked. I didn't look long but his back and arms were full of huge red bumps and sores. Something is wrong! This isn't right!"

Then I said, "Well we gotta go get help. We gotta go find some help."

Joe said, "Get help? Bro, what do you mean go get help? We can't just leave him here."

Then Tim chimed in and said, "Well what do y'all think we should do? we can't just sit here and wait for whoever's with him to come back. We gotta get outta here!"

Joe added frantically, "But we can't just leave the kid."

Then I whispered, "If we take the kid, that's kidnapping, and I don't know about that. I don't think we should take the kid."

Joe said, "Well I'm not gonna leave the kid. He's coming with us. We not leaving a naked kid in an empty tent in the

77

middle of the woods. I'll go get him. And when I get him, we're gonna have to run like hell to get outta here."

We all shook our heads in agreement. We knew Joe was doing the right thing. As much as we all wanted to turn and run back to the tracks, we knew we couldn't leave the boy. So, we watched with great intensity as Joe approached the tent.

Unlike Tim's approach, Joe moved quickly. Within seconds he went in the tent and came out running and carrying the small naked boy. I couldn't believe what was happening. This was crazy. This was the craziest and scariest thing in my whole life.

As Joe approached us, I could see the boy's body was covered with red sores. He was half asleep and thin and couldn't have been more than three to four years old. Joe said, "I got him. Now let's go. We gotta get outta here." As Joe ran with the boy, we all stayed close together. We were all running fast. So fast that I wondered how long we could keep up this pace. We had a long way to go to get back to the tracks, and I knew at some point we would have to slow down.

But for now, we were moving through the woods at a rabbit's pace. Our fears pushed us and outweighed any and all fatigue. But the shaking and rough movement had startled the child and soon after we started running, he awoke and began to cry.

First it was a small whimper but then his cries became louder and louder. And hearing the boy's cry terrified me. It made everything worse. It made an intense moment almost unbearable. But Joe kept running and seemed unphased by the boy's cries.

As Joe ran, he continued his pace and held the boy tight. And as we ran, the small dog ran alongside us. It was a scene and moment that none of us would forget.

78

Three teenage black boys running through the woods carrying a small naked white child, with a small yellow dog running beside us.

Within no time we reached the shallow creek. The same creek where Larry had been waiting. And when he saw us running toward him, he stood up and looked as if he had seen a ghost. I can only imagine what he was thinking when he saw us running full speed back across the creek with Joe carrying a small, naked child.

But before Larry could ask what was going on, Joe had run right past him, and the small dog was keeping pace running alongside him. Larry was startled but quickly gathered himself and started to run with us. I ran right to him and said, "Larry, we gotta get outta here! We have to go."

Then I grabbed and pulled his shirt and tried to get him to run faster. "We gotta get outta these woods! We found the boy. He was alone in a tent. He needs help. You gotta run faster bro."

Larry said, "What do you mean y'all found him? You don't just find a kid in the middle of the woods. What the heck is wrong with y'all? How you go from finding puppies to finding a naked kid?"

I said, "You need to keep up bro. We got a long way to go."

Then Larry complained, "But I can't run that far. I gotta walk. Joe and Tim are already gone… they way up there. Walk with me bro. I can't make it running like this." So then, Larry slowed down. Then he stopped running, hunched over and tried to catch his breath.

He didn't even run fifty yards. He was overweight, out of breath and tired. I tried to walk with him, but he seemed like he was having problems. That short burst of running had taken all of his energy. He was done and we were a long, long way from the tracks.

I stayed back and speed walked with Larry until I heard a sound that forced me to run away and leave him. It was a loud voice from behind me that was hollering for us to stop. It was a man's voice and along with his commands for us to stop were the sounds of crackling leaves and fast-moving footsteps.

The footsteps were approaching from a distance in the woods. Then the man's commands to stop became louder and angrier, and from the sounds of the crackling leaves he was getting closer and closer. I knew I couldn't speed walk with Larry any longer. I had to leave him.

I didn't say a word to him. I just took off and ran away from him as fast as I could. When I left Larry behind, I never looked back. And not soon after I left him, I heard what appeared to be a loud plea from Larry.

He cried out, "No! Please. Don't!" And then I heard two loud gunshots. Then there was a brief pause from the sound of crackling leaves. I knew the man had shot Larry and was probably standing over him.

Then the sound of fast-moving footsteps and crackling leaves continued as well as an even angrier command for us to stop running. The angry commands to stop, and the sounds of footsteps were daunting and frightening.

But nothing compared to the sound of the bullets I soon heard as they whizzed past my head. The man was firing shots at us and all we could do was run. I ran as fast as I could and hoped I wouldn't get hit.

I don't know that I ever run that fast in my life. I ran so fast that I almost caught up to Tim and Mark who were now only a few yards ahead of me. We had been running for what seemed like forever, and the train tracks were not that far away. Maybe two hundred yards, maybe less... we were close, very close.

And the closer we got to the tracks, the more shots the man fired. As I continued to run, I felt the breeze of another bullet as it zipped by my head. Fortunately, the bullet missed me, but unfortunately it hit Tim. He was running a few yards in front of me.

When the bullet hit him, he immediately fell face down in the leaves under his feet. I wanted to help him, but I couldn't stop. I continued running and ran right past him. I was consumed by fear, and I kept running.

And then a few seconds later I heard another shot. It was a single shot that I knew he used to finish off Tim. Sadly, me and Joe were the only two left running. And the man firing at us wasn't far behind. He was close. The sounds of footsteps behind me grew closer and closer.

By now Joe was nearing the train tracks and I was not far behind. As Joe ran through the woods he zigzagged and tried to avoid making himself an easy target. But just as Joe hit the opening in the woods, with the train tracks in clear view, the man opened fire again with another barrage of gunshots.

And this time none of them whizzed by me. They weren't meant for me. They were all intended for Joe. And they hit their target with precision. I helplessly watched as Joe was shot in the back and tragically fell to the ground. As he stumbled, he dropped from his arms the small child he had been carrying through the woods.

Without hesitation I ran toward Joe, grabbed the small boy by his arm, then yanked and pulled him from the ground toward my chest. And with him firmly in my arms I dashed across the tracks. I couldn't let him be taken back into the woods.

All of my friends had been shot and I was the only hope to save the boy and myself. I had to get to the other side of the tracks. That was the only thing I could think of. I knew I had to make it.

And as I ran across the tracks, I could feel the commanding voice and footsteps behind me get closer and closer. I didn't think I would make it. My heart was beating so hard that I thought it would burst from my chest. The boy held me close. His grip was tight. It was as if he knew I was his protector.

Then I heard what I thought were the last sounds my ears would hear. It was one, then two and then three more loud gunshots. I kept running and somehow, I reached the edge of the woods on the other side of the tracks. I couldn't believe I hadn't been hit.

Then out of nowhere, while running and carrying the boy, I tripped over a large stick hidden in the brush and fell hard to the ground. The naked boy I was carrying fell next to me. Everything was quiet. Almost too quiet.

I didn't know what was going on, and I was afraid to move. But then, after a few seconds of lying on the ground, I poked my head up from where I had fallen. I didn't hear any more gunshots or footsteps approaching me from behind. It was eerily quiet. Then as I lifted my head up from the woods, I heard a familiar voice in the background.

Not the one yelling out commands and firing bullets at me. This was a welcoming voice. It was the voice of one of 'the older boys.' He was only a few yards away from me and he was hunched down in the woods. Next to him were three other boys, all of them were older boys.

Chapter 11

The Older Boys

Somehow when I came out of the woods and ran across the train tracks, I ran right into them. I couldn't believe it. Out of all the places I could have run, I ran to the almost exact spot they were at in the woods.

One of the older boys hunched down next to me was Joe's older brother Wayne. In his hand was a gun. He had fired the four or five shots I heard as I was running across the tracks. He fired the shots that ended the deadly pursuit.

As I looked through the woods toward the train tracks, I could see the body of the man from the woods. Joe's brother had shot the man who had shot all of my friends and tried to kill me. One of the other boys looked at me with shock in his eyes and exclaimed, "What the hell did you guys get into!? And why are you running through the woods with a naked kid!?"

And then another one asked, "Why was that man tryna kill you!?"
I shook my head and pitifully whined, "I don't know. I don't know who he is, but we need to get help. They in the woods. He shot everybody. He shot Larry, Tim and Joe. He shot all of them. But I think Joe may be alive. He fell on the edge of the woods. Right off the tracks over there. I think he may be alive!"

Then all the older boys rose up from the woods and ran toward Joe. Two of them were Joe's older brothers. And as they ran toward Joe the man from the woods' body began to move. Surprisingly, he wasn't dead and slowly turned his head in their direction. When Joe's brother saw the man moving, he walked toward him and fired another shot. Now the man from the woods was definitely dead.

After watching him shoot the man, I stood up and grabbed the small boy again. By now all the older boys had run over and were tending to Joe. I didn't follow in their direction. I picked up the boy and carried him through the small stretch of woods that led to our homes.

As I pierced through the woods, the first person I saw was a sheriff's deputy. He heard a shot fired alert and responded by arriving in the area. I immediately ran toward him carrying the naked boy in my arms. As I got close to him the magnitude of what had just happened weighed on me and I began to cry, almost uncontrollably.

I cried because I was glad to be alive. I cried because I made it. Somehow, I had made it out of those woods.

One of our neighbors who was standing next to the police officer took a picture of me coming out of the woods carrying the naked child. Within a few hours, that picture would be shown on almost every news station across the country and was soon to be on the cover of every major magazine in the U.S. As the horrible events of that day were reported, it became one of the biggest stories in the world.

I learned that the boy we found in the woods had been missing for almost six months. He was from a small town about five hours and three states from the woods where we found him. His mother said she was in the backyard hanging clothes when he disappeared. She said she had only been away for fifteen minutes and had left the boy in the house watching TV.

The boy apparently opened the front door of his home so the dog could run outside. The boy's mother said when she went back inside the house both the boy and the dog were gone. As fate would have it, the dog he let out the house just so happened to be the same dog he was with in the woods.

The same dog that led us to him. That small yellow dog turned out to be his hero. And when people found out about the heroic dog, hearts were warmed all over the world. But as the dog had warmed hearts with her heroism, the man in the woods had pierced them with his evil acts.

As the investigation unfolded, it was discovered that the man in the woods was a disturbed man. He was a homeless war veteran who drifted from town to town looking for work. He had only been in the boy's town for a day when he stumbled on the boy and his pregnant dog playing in their front yard. No one knows why he kidnapped the boy and his dog or why he took them to live deep in the isolated woods where they were found.

And because he was dead no one would ever know what transpired during the boy's captivity. Before his kidnapping the boy was a vibrant four-year-old who loved to play with his dog and sing along to his favorite A, B, C melodies. But when he returned from the woods, he was a speechless and emotionless child.

The doctors diagnosed him with having selective mutism which meant the boy was able to speak but chose not to. And other than the sounds he made when crying, the boy made no attempts whatsoever to communicate. His life would never be the same.

Chapter 12

Too Many Losses

That heroic day and those horrific events changed our lives forever. Two of my friends had died at the hands of the man in the woods. Both Tim and Larry were gone. And Joe, though he survived, would never be the same.

Joe was shot in the back by a bullet that barely missed his spine. He was gravely injured, and his football days were over. Both the physical and psychological pain he endured would last for years.

I only spoke to Joe once since that day in the woods. After everything that happened it was rare for either of us to be seen out in public or to leave our homes for an extended period of time. It would be weeks before I returned to school and Joe, with football off the table, he never returned at all. He dropped out. Just like his two older brothers before him, he dropped out of school.

The one time I did see him our conversation was brief. I was riding in the car with my mother, and I saw Joe at the gas station. He was leaving while I was entering. We didn't say much. We both put our fists out for a fist bump, then hugged each other.

When I asked Joe if he was okay and he said, "I'm not okay, but I'm alive." And that was it. That's all we said to each other. He then turned away and walked to his brother's car.

And when he turned and walked away, I could see he had a noticeable limp in his walk. But other than that, he looked great. Joe looked like he was living his life as best he could.

He was clean, neat, and appeared normal. But deep inside Joe was broken. I heard from several people that Joe was having a hard time coming to grips with his new limitations. They say Joe was very depressed, but he refused to get help or go to counseling.

I was fortunate that my scars were all but invisible. I kept them tucked away and hidden inside my mind. But Joe wore his scars every day. You could see the pain in his eyes and his scars were visible when he walked.

And Tim and Larry's scars got buried with them. The bullets that took them out are forever implanted in their bodies deep in their graves. And our town had some scars too. After that day, our town would never be the same.

TV cameras, news reports, detectives and FBI agents were everywhere. They were talking to townspeople, our teachers, and our neighbors. They talked to anyone who wanted to talk to them. Anyone who could give them a glimpse into our town and the young men who risked their lives saving a young stranger.

Later we learned there had been a reward for the boy's safe return. It wasn't a lot of money and they offered to give it to me and Joe. But I demanded that the money be split with Tim and Larry's families as well. After the reward money was split four ways it wasn't much money at all. But I knew that was the right thing to do.

And people offered me and Joe tons of money to do interviews, but neither of us did. They all wanted details. One guy offered us a million dollars each if we sat down with him to write a book, but we turned that down too. We weren't looking to make money off what happened to our friends or what we went through that day. We just wanted to move on. And people just couldn't understand that.

And that's how things went. That day in the woods I learned that survival is a natural instinct. We instinctively chose that on that day that the young boy would live. That he would survive. But ultimately those instincts lead to the deaths of two of my friends and a horrible man from the woods.

As the years went by and the events of that day moved further and further to the back of my mind, I couldn't help but wonder what happened to the young boy we saved. So many lives were changed that day. I had hoped the boy was living a good life but deep inside I knew his life would be a struggle. He had gone through too much to ever be a normal kid again.

But my curiosity got the best of me. I wanted to know how he was doing so I Googled his name. I was hoping that someone would have written an update on his life. But when I searched for him an article about Joe popped up.

It said, 'Man who years ago rescued a small boy from the woods takes own life.' And sadly, that's how I learned about Joe. The article said that on a cold rainy morning Joe went and revisited the train tracks where our lives had been forever changed. He then stood at the exact spot where he laid on the ground after he had been shot in the back, then he took out a revolver and took his own life.

It was a tragic ending for Joe. A man who as a kid had so much potential. He was my friend and I missed him dearly. But I knew Joe could never come to grips with the way his life had turned out. I certainly didn't agree with Joe taking his own life, but I understood why he did it.

With Joe's passing all three of my childhood friends had died. I often wondered what life would have been like if we never followed that dog into the woods. If we never crossed that creek. And if we never went and pulled the boy from the tent.

But in spite of everything, I don't regret the decision we made. Sometimes our instincts make us do things that we later regret. And as bad as things turned out, I didn't regret saving the boy's life.

So, after everything that happened my mother waited for me to finish the last three months of school and then we moved. We moved to a small town several hours away. When my father died, he left my mother with an insurance policy that meant she would never have to work again. And she didn't. She lived a modest life and did as best she could take care of me and my sister.

My sister would eventually find a job in our new town, and I enrolled in my new school. But everything was different. There was no coming home and hanging with my friends. There was no more running through the woods. No more cracking jokes with fat Larry. All those days were gone.

From then on, I stuck to myself. I wasn't interested in meeting new people, and I certainly wasn't interested in meeting new friends. I wasn't really interested in anything. My life had become routine, boring and sad.

And then one day my mother gave me a journal. She told me I could write in it whatever I wanted. She said writing would make me feel better and it would be a way for me to share my thoughts. So, I started writing. And she was right. I felt much better. And the first thing I wrote about were the events of that day. I wrote a short story about the events of that day, and I called it 'The Older Boys.' I called it that because those older boys had saved my life. They are the reason I have a passion for writing.

Chapter 13

Sent Mail

After reading over the story, I had written years ago I opened my email and typed Diana's email address in the 'send to' line. I typed 'My Story' in the subject line and I sent her an attachment of my story. When Diana checked her email, she would read my story and we would have a ton to discuss. The story I wrote was unique and dear to me I knew she would enjoy reading it.

After reading everything over I grew very tired and immediately fell asleep. I had a very eventful day, and my mind and body were physically and mentally exhausted. The next morning when I woke up the first thing, I did was grab my computer to check my email. I wanted to see if Diana had read my story and responded.

But when I checked my email inbox nothing was there. Diana had not responded. I thought that was odd, so I checked my sent mail to double check if I had sent it to the right email address. But when I went to my sent mail, strangely there was no trace of the email I had sent to Diana.

I searched hard but couldn't find the email I had just sent her last night. There was no email titled 'My Story' and there were no attachments titled 'The Older Boys.'

Then I checked my work email to see if maybe I had sent it from there but surprisingly nothing was there either. I was puzzled. I thought to myself that maybe I had fallen asleep and never sent it. I was very tired last night.

Or maybe I had titled it something else. Or maybe I sent it from a different email account. I had all kinds of thoughts and scenarios in my head but at the end of the day I knew I emailed Diana my story from my personal email account, and I knew I sent it to the email she gave me. The one she wrote down on a piece of paper and gave me at Starbucks. So, then I took the next step and looked for the paper I had where she wrote down her email address.

Last night I had placed it on the coffee table next to my laptop. But strangely, that paper wasn't there either. I then looked all over the place. I searched both couches and then checked both coffee tables. I must have looked all over my apartment, but I couldn't find that paper with her email address.

And now I was really starting to feel worried. I tried to back track and remember everything I had done last night. The last thing I remembered doing before I sent the email was grabbing a bottle of water from the fridge. Maybe I left the paper with her email address on the kitchen counter. I was sure that's where it was, so I headed to the kitchen to find it.

But when I turned the lights on in the kitchen, I didn't see the paper I was looking for. That's not what I saw. But what I did see was a long steady column of ants walking across my counters. The same kitchen counter I had sprayed with ant spray the day before. The same kitchen counter that I sprayed with a bug spray that all but guaranteed to keep the ants away.

How could the ants be back? I had just sprayed the counters last night. And here they were proudly parading on my counters again. I was frustrated and confused. And when I opened the cabinet door where I kept my various chemicals, mosquito repellent and bug spray, there was no bug spray to be found. Nothing but cans of air freshener.

There was no trace of the odorless bug spray I had bought just the day before.

It became very clear to me that something was not right. Something was definitely wrong with this picture, and I was determined to find out what it was. To make matters worse, when I looked in my phone for Diana's phone number, I couldn't find that either. When I checked my phone contacts her number was nowhere to be found.

Somehow Diana's phone number had been erased from my phone contacts and her email address had been erased from my sent mail. On top of that, the paper she gave me with her contact information was gone as well. And not to be outdone were the seemingly defiant ants in my kitchen that were back parading on my counters with no trace of the bug spray I bought the day before.

As strange as everything seemed I had no choice but to assume that maybe Diana was somehow nothing more than a figure in my dream. It must have all been a dream. There was no other explanation. I must have dreamt about her and everything in between.

But everything seemed so real. Diana was special. She was lovely and she was perfect, and we connected almost as soon as we saw each other. I felt a bond with her. I had fallen for her, and she had fallen for me.

When she placed her hand on top of mine and asked me to feel her energy, we made a connection. I hoped and prayed she wasn't just a beautiful figure from my imagination. I liked her and I needed her to be real.

I decided the only thing left for me to do to verify if she was real was to go to the Starbucks and see if she showed up. Yesterday we had planned a second meeting there. We agreed to meet there today at 4:30 p.m. If she showed up all my anxiety and fears would be erased. But if she didn't… Well, I didn't want to think about that.

At this point all I could do was hope for the best. There was nothing else I could do. So that whole day all I did was sit around and think about Diana. And even though I just talked to her yesterday I already missed her dearly. This was going to be a long day and 4:30 wouldn't get here fast enough.

And the day dragged on; it moved at what seemed like a turtle's pace. My mind was all over the place. At first, I was nervous and worried and then I became tireless and anxious. I must have aged ten years that day as the stress of watching the clock took its toll on me.

For almost the whole day I did absolutely nothing. Nothing but hope time would fly by as quickly as possible. But it never did. I had to wait and watch the clock for each painstaking minute and every painstaking hour. It was the longest day of my life.

As the hours went by, I wrote down as many things about Diana as I could remember. I wrote down her name – Diana Johnson, her address – 910 Blue Heart Lane. Then I wrote down what I could remember about her schedule.

Monday and Tuesday she did this and Wednesday and Thursday she did that. I wrote down what she said about her mother and her mother's passing. Then I wrote down what I remembered about her grandmother. I wrote notes on everything about her that I could think of. And then finally, as the day inched along, 4:30 finally neared so I headed out the door to Starbucks.

Chapter 14

Searching for Answers

Yesterday she had gotten there before me, and I was hoping today she would beat me there again. But when I got to Starbucks I walked in and looked to the left and then to the right, but I didn't see Diana. I thought to myself, well I must have beat her there. So I took a seat next to the door at the exact same table we sat at yesterday and waited.

When I glanced at my watch, I realized I was early. It was only 4 p.m. and we weren't scheduled to meet until 4:30. I had a little time to wait so I motioned the waitress over and ordered a large chocolate latte. I told her I was waiting on a guest and that she didn't need to check on me for at least thirty minutes.

Then at 4:30 the waitress came back to my table and gave me a refill. And then fifteen minutes later at 4:45 she came back for a third time. By now I had been sitting alone at the table for forty-five minutes and had miserably drunk three large chocolate lattes. When 5 p.m. came around Diana was nowhere in sight, and I knew it was time for me to leave.

I had been sitting alone at the table for over an hour. My time was up. I knew she wasn't coming. When I motioned for the waitress and asked for my bill my face was full of disappointment. I felt terrible and the waitress could tell I was distraught.

When she handed me my bill, she asked me if I was okay. She said, "I sure hate that your friend never showed up. I see that happen a lot here. People supposed to meet up and then the other person doesn't show. Somebody's always going home disappointed in this place. But you gotta keep your head up. She may have a good reason. Things happen you know."

I nodded my head in agreement and asked her a few questions.

"How often do you work at this place?"

She said, "I work here every day. Every day from 12 to 8 p.m."

"Oh really" I said, "Because my lady friend comes here all the time. Every Tuesday at 4 p.m. And when she comes here, she sits right here at this table and reads her books. And she was here yesterday. And I was sitting here with her. We were sitting right here at this table. She was supposed to meet me here today, but she didn't show up."

Then the waitress responded "Baby I don't remember her. I work here every day and I know all my regulars. I'm the only person that works the floor. Outside of the cooks, I run this place. I know everybody that comes through the door because I make, they drinks. Tuesdays are my slowest days and I aint got no regulars on Tuesdays.

"I'm sorry but I don't remember her and as a matter of fact I don't remember you either. I don't remember either one of y'all sitting at this table yesterday. I would know cause yesterday it was slow and aint nobody come in here after three. It was so slow that I stepped outside and made a few personal phone calls, and it didn't get busy till well after 5. Y'all must have gone to another store because you didn't come here."

I nodded my head in agreement and thanked her for her time. Then I walked out and went back to my car where I sat quietly and processed what she told me. I couldn't believe what was happening. Diana was not only a no show

95

for our second meeting, but the waitress said she didn't remember her. Diana told me she went there faithfully every Tuesday, but the waitress said otherwise.

And not only did she say she didn't remember Diana, but she also said she didn't remember me being there yesterday either. I was sitting at the table with Diana, and we must have talked for close to an hour. But I wasn't sure if the waitress was there yesterday or not. I wasn't paying attention to anybody but Diana.

If she doesn't remember me, well that's okay cause I don't remember her either. But Diana said she went there every Tuesday. It was strange and puzzling that the waitress couldn't remember one of her regular customers.

Everything seemed to be falling apart. Maybe I had been dreaming. There was simply no other explanation. Last night I was excited and anxious and today I was worried and confused. When I got home, I vowed to get to the bottom of this. I couldn't explain what was happening, but I was determined to find an explanation.

So the first thing I did was I took out the piece of paper that had all the things I had written down about Diana and then I went to work. I searched for Diana Johnson's name on Facebook hoping to find her but quickly realized it was a time consuming and fruitless task. There were absolutely tons of women with her same name. There must have been a thousand profiles of Diana Johnsons in the Atlanta area alone.

There were white Diana's and black Diana's. Tall Diana's and short Diana's. All types of Diana's and they lived all over the place. Then I searched other forms of social media sites but still had no luck. I searched Instagram, Twitter, and LinkedIn. I searched them all, but I couldn't find anything.

I looked at hundreds of profiles but came up empty. I knew another approach was needed. I had to find a way to narrow down my search. So instead of searching for her name I searched for her address. I could never forget that. It was 910 Blue Heart Lane. And when I searched for that address things got very interesting.

At first, I didn't see any properties that matched that address. There was a 910 Blue Bonnet Lane, a 910 Blue Hills Lane, a 910 Bluebird Lane and several other 910 Blue Somethings but nothing that matched what I was looking for. I searched all over Georgia but that address simply didn't exist.

But I wasn't giving up. Next, I searched for that address in nearby Tennessee, but I got the same results. There were no exact matches. But I continued searching and expanded my search to properties in South Carolina, North Carolina, Florida and all the other states that neared my home state of Georgia. I searched them all and painfully nothing jumped out.

I was tired and disappointed and almost gave up. Then it happened. A few states away, all the way in Missouri there was a 910 Blue Heart Lane. I couldn't believe it. After hours of searching, I had finally found a property that matched the address Diana had given me.

There wasn't much information about the house on the website but when I looked closer, I noticed a small, almost hidden, link on the bottom of the page. And when I clicked on that link, I was taken to the Missouri County property appraiser's website. And that's where I finally found what I was looking for.

The home on 910 Blue Heart Lane in Missouri County, Missouri was listed as having two owners. One was a person named Olive Johnson and the other was a person named Diana Johnson. The records show that Olive Johnson had purchased the home nearly forty years ago and then five years ago the title had been transferred to Diana Johnson. The home had three bedrooms, two bathrooms and a one car garage.

Diana had shared with me that after her grandmother had passed away, she received a call from an attorney. The attorney told her that she had been gifted a home. Now everything was making sense. Everything was adding up.

I knew then that Olive had to be her grandmother. She had to be. There was no other explanation.

Before Olive died, she left Diana her home on 910 Blue Heart Lane. That was the house she told me that her and her son turned into their home. She told me it was a place where she could love him and then one day, she could leave for him. I was onto something here. I wasn't gonna stop until I figured this out.

After finding this information I knew exactly what I had to do. I had to go to 910 Blue Heart Lane to see it for myself. I had to take a road trip to see if this was Diana's home in Missouri County, Missouri.

It was a seven-hour drive away and I was ready to hit the road to see it. I was anxious. So much so that I decided that tomorrow I would make my move. Tomorrow I would travel to 910 Blue Heart Lane in Missouri County, Missouri. I was determined to find Diana, and this was my best path to do so.

The next morning, I got up and packed a small overnight bag, and prepared for my road trip. I knew this was going to be a very spontaneous move that I hadn't really thought through. I didn't really know where I was going or what I would do once I got there. I just knew I had to go.

I booked a hotel for one night in Missouri County and planned to only stay for one day. When I looked at my watch it was 9.00 a.m., and I was ready to hit the road. The drive

98

would take about seven hours which meant I would arrive at the home on Blue Heart Lane around 4 p.m. I had no idea what to expect when I got there but that didn't matter. The only thing I knew was this road trip had the potential to be a fascinating experience and I was excited to start my journey.

Chapter 15

Road Trip

If Diana turned out to be real, this could be the single most important event in my life. This was big. Really big. The whole time I was on the road all I could think about was getting there as quickly as I could.

My drive there was peaceful and relaxing, and after seven hours I arrived on schedule at the town of Missouri County, Missouri. It was a small town and was kinda what I had pictured it to be in my head. There wasn't a whole lot of traffic, and it seemed like a safe town. There were no large apartment complexes or glamorous high-rise buildings. This was a small rural town that felt like a nice place to live.

I drove by several small, older neighborhoods that were tucked away off the sides of the main road that cut through the town. This was an older town and there weren't a lot of new buildings or nice things to see, but it kinda reminded me of my home in Georgia. It just felt like a nice place to live.

When I arrived in town the first thing I did was check into my hotel. After that I drove around the town to get a better feel of the community. I knew somewhere in this town there was a Diana Johnson and I hoped and prayed she was the woman of my dreams. I hoped she was the woman I came all this way looking for. I was nervous, excited, and determined to find her.

While driving around I noticed there was a Publix directly across the street from my hotel. It was the only large grocery store in town. There was also a small public library in a shopping plaza about a mile or so down the road. This is important because I knew Diana followed a very detailed schedule.

She told me she always shopped at Publix on Mondays and then took her son to the library on Wednesdays. Today was Wednesday. So, if things panned out like I hoped, I knew just where to find Diana later in the afternoon.

As I continued driving around the small town, I couldn't help but think about what was happening. I had so many questions and thoughts in my head. Would Diana be the beautiful woman from my dream or someone different? Would she be as nice, caring, and compassionate as the woman in my dream?

Would she immediately recognize me, or would I be a stranger? What would I do if she recognized me and what would I do if she didn't? What would I say to her? What would she say to me?

While driving around town my anxiety began to increase. I had all kinds of thoughts zipping in and out of my head. I knew I had to refocus and contain myself.

I had to focus on one thing at a time. I had to focus on my first move and then my next. And my first step was to drive by her home to see if she actually lived there.

So, I put 910 Blue Heart Lane in my GPS and followed the directions. Surprisingly, her home was close. It was actually very close. It was less than ten minutes away.

I had just arrived in this town and now I was only ten minutes away from my destination. As I drove toward her home, I got so nervous that I had to pull over on the side of the road to catch my breath.

I had to gather myself. In a matter of minutes, I would be parked directly in front of her house. I had to ready myself. The clock was ticking, and the time was now.

An abundance of questions and thoughts all reappeared in my mind. What would I do when I pulled up and parked in front of her home? Should I get out of my car and go knock on the door, or should I sit in my car and wait for her to come home? I hadn't prepared for this. At this point I really didn't know what I would do. But I figured I would cross that bridge when I got to it, so I continued driving.

After a short while I arrived at 910 Blue Heart Lane. I pulled off to the right on the street then rolled my windows down and took in the sights and smells of the neighborhood. There was a calming feeling of peace and tranquility.

All the homes on her street had nice lawns that were all well maintained. The yards were cut, and their bushes and hedges were neatly trimmed. The cars in front of the homes were all neatly parked in their driveways. A few of the houses had clothes lines that strung across their front yards and there was a pleasant smell of fresh linen blowing in the wind.

Having never been to this place before it had the feel of a place where older people might reside. Maybe retired people. This place was really quiet and felt safe and peaceful.

Almost all of the homes on this street were older and were probably built many years ago. Some of the cars in the driveways were older as well. And on several of the porches I saw plants, flowers, wind chimes and even rocking chairs.

This was definitely a community of seniors. Diana's grandmother could absolutely have lived on a street like this. 910 Blue Heart Lane was two houses up from where I had parked and there were no cars in the driveway.

I cautiously got out of my car and walked up to the home to take a closer look. There was no need for me to be nervous about walking up to the house. Everything here was quiet and peaceful. My plan was to walk up to the front porch and look around.

910 Blue Heart Lane was a small brown house. It had a one car garage and a one car driveway. It had a small porch with modern patio furniture and a few wind chimes that hung from above.

All the curtains and windows around the home were closed so there was no way for me to see inside. Diana had never described her home to me, so I had no way of knowing if she lived here or not. I wasn't mentally prepared to knock on the door so I figured the best thing I could do was to wait in my car until later this evening when she and her son came home.

I parked my car down the street a few houses down, but it was close enough that I could see Diana when she returned home. As I sat in my car thinking, I realized Diana might not be home for several hours. It was 4:30 p.m. and they might not be home until well after 6 or 7 p.m.

And by that time, it would be dark outside and I wouldn't be able to get a good look at her. I realized waiting until later was not a good idea. I had to think of something. I had to think of other options, so I pulled out my notes and I reviewed the things I had written down about Diana.

One thing I focused on a lot was her schedule. How detailed she was about following routines. One thing that jumped out to me was on Fridays she said she would let her son ride the bus home from school. She wanted to teach him to be confident and independent. She said sometimes she would meet him at the bus stop and other times she would watch him from the blinds in her home.

She said she would wait for him to enter the house and then when he came in, she would give him a big welcoming hug. I dissected this information in my head, and I came away with a few conclusions.

First, Diana's son probably didn't have a key to her home. He didn't need one. He was only six and he rode to school with his mother every day. He only rode the school bus home one day a week on Fridays. So, he didn't need a key.

Second, on the days he rode the bus home I was pretty sure Diana left a key under the mat for him. She wanted to teach him independence. If he didn't carry a key, which I assumed he didn't, he had to have a way to get into the home. She mentioned waiting for him to open the door and then giving him a big hug, so I knew he had to have a way to get in.

Third, I think I found a way to get into her home. All I needed to do was look for a key under the mat. This was a safe community, and I was pretty sure Diana had no worries about leaving a key under the mat.

Feeling confident that I could get into her home, I got out of my car and walked over to her house again. I was sure a key was under the mat. If it was, I needed to get in and get out as quickly as possible. I wasn't planning on being inside long. Just long enough to confirm if she lived there or not.

When I walked up to the porch, I lifted the mat in front of the door and just as I had predicted, there was a small silver key. I reached down and grabbed it and quickly opened the door. When I entered the house the sweet smell of women's perfume was present.

The smell reminded me of Diana. It was a smooth, clean, and peachy smell that satisfied my senses. But I needed more proof than just a familiar fragrance.

I needed proof that she lived here. And fortunately for me it didn't take long for me to find it. Because sitting right smack in front of me on an end table was a small stack of pictures. Pictures of the women who lived in this house.

And sure enough they were pictures of the person I had hoped to find. In front of me was a treasure chest of pictures of Diana and her son. It was definitely her. She was in all the pictures. She was real, she was beautiful, and she most definitely lived in this house.

I was overcome with relief. It was a beautiful feeling to know that my hunch was correct. That Diana was too real to only exist in my dreams. The pictures of Diana made my heart pump with pride. I was pleased to know I had gotten it right.

Now the only thing I needed to do was get out of her home before I got caught. I didn't have permission to be here, and it would be impossible for me to explain why I was there. But before I left, I took out my phone and took a couple pictures of the pictures on the end table.

While taking pictures of the pictures on the end table I noticed there were even more pictures on the adjacent end table, so I went over and glanced at a few of them as well. But these pictures were different. Very different.

At first, I couldn't believe what I saw. On the other end table were several more pictures of Diana, but in these pictures, she was with another man. Pictures of a man hugging and holding hands with her. The pictures seemed to be of her and a companion.

But what made the pictures strange was the fact that the man in the pictures looked a lot like me. If I didn't know better, I would think the pictures *were* of me. There were pictures of this man with Diana and also pictures of him posing by himself. I couldn't understand it.

Who was this guy and why did he resemble me? I didn't know what his connection was to Diana, but it clearly looked like they were in some type of relationship. And next to the pictures was a small 'thinking of you' card with a handwritten note.

It said: Hey Diana. Just sharing a reminder that I will be on jury duty for about two weeks. I leave on Wednesday and will return next Saturday. I have been picked to be on a jury in Jefferson County. They haven't told me much, but I hear it's a really big case. Unfortunately, I can't talk to you while I'm away so I will see you when I return. I will be thinking about you while I'm gone. Take care.

And the card had the man's signature scribbled at the bottom. I couldn't make it out and I had no clue who this guy was. The only thing I knew was he was going to be a juror in Jefferson County. I didn't know anything about Jefferson County other than that I drove through it on my way to Diana's home and it was about two hours away. With this new information I knew that at some point I would probably be heading to Jefferson County for more answers.

Chapter 16

The Library

And as for Diana, after seeing pictures of her and this mysterious man my mood changed. I went from feeling thrilled that I had found her to feeling confused with not knowing who the man was in the pictures. Before I left, I snapped a couple of pictures of the mysterious man and then I got out of the house, thankfully without being noticed.

Having confirmed that Diana lived at the home and was in fact a real person I sat in my car and debriefed. I contemplated my next move. According to my notes, Diana followed a daily routine and on this day her and her son were scheduled to be at the library.

From what she told me when we met at Starbucks, every Wednesday they went to the library. And the library was only a short way away. If I wanted to see her, that was my best option.

According to my notes she was all but guaranteed to be there. With the exception of the mystery man, everything seemed to be going as I had hoped. If my luck continued, in a very short period of time I would get another opportunity to lay my eyes on Diana.

Now it was officially gametime. I knew I had to be ready. As I drove off in my car, I contemplated two different scenarios I might encounter at the library. In one scenario Diana would recognize me and in the other she wouldn't. I had to have a plan for both, because in all honesty I had no idea what would happen if and when I saw her.

If she didn't recognize me, all bets were off. I would have traveled here for nothing. I quickly canceled those thoughts and moved to the next scenario. The best thing I could do was plan for her recognizing me.

This wouldn't be an unexpected meeting of strangers like the one we had at the grocery store. When she saw me, I had to plan on her instantly recognizing me. And once she did our conversation would evolve from there.

Diana followed a detailed almost ritualistic schedule, and I knew she would be at the library. There was no way I could make it seem like I just happened to be there or like I didn't know she would be there.

I knew that wouldn't work. When I saw her, the easiest thing for me to do would be to walk up to her, say hello and then give her a good reason for me being there.

Since I looked so much like the mysterious man in the pictures at her home my plan was to act like I was him. And as much as I tried, I simply couldn't understand why he looked so much like me. Pretending to be him was not something I looked forward to doing but it was my best, worst option.

Whoever that man was, hopefully she would think I was him and she would welcome me. And the more and more I thought about this plan, the more confident I became. It seemed like something that could work.

The message written on the card at her home said the man in the pictures would begin his jury duty today. It was currently 5 p.m. so there was still time for me to come up with a story that allowed me to explain why I was still in town and had not reported to jury duty two hours away in Jefferson County. I anticipated Diana would wonder why I hadn't yet left.

108

I needed to come up with a reason why I was still in town. Luckily, I was able to think of a reason that I thought would work. I would tell her that I had left an important piece of identification that I needed to check in for jury duty.

I would tell her that the courthouse required jurors to present two forms of ID and I had carelessly only brought one. I would tell her that somehow, I forgot to bring my social security card which I left on the bedroom dresser. At the courthouse I realized I didn't have it and had to drive all the way back home to get it.

I would tell her the court gave me until 8 p.m. tonight to get back to the courthouse to check in, and while I was back in town, I decided to stop by the library to see her before I left again. That was it. That was my story, and I liked the way it sounded.

It seemed like a story that most anyone would believe. But as confident as I was, I also knew there were other things I needed to focus on for this to work. First, I had no idea who the man was in the pictures. I was planning to impersonate someone I had never met. Pretend to be someone I had never seen.

What if we looked alike but talked differently? What if my voice was deeper than his or his was deeper than mine? What if he was taller than me, or heavier than me?

And then what if our personalities were different? What if he laughed and smiled a lot and I was the serious type? I didn't know anything about him. How could I possibly pretend to be someone based solely on how they looked in a picture?

Suddenly I didn't feel as good with my last-minute plan as I did a few minutes earlier. I was becoming worried. And there were a ton of other things I didn't know.

Like what kinda car the guy drove. What if at the library Diana says, "Well thanks for stopping by, let me walk you out." What kinda car would I walk her to? And then there were other big and little issues to deal with. Tons of them. So many that I decided to ignore them and proceed with my original plan.

I had to clear my thoughts. I couldn't worry about things I can't control. If I did, they would only make me more paranoid and cause me to overthink an already fragile situation. I didn't want to make this more complicated than it already was.

This wasn't a meet and greet lunch date. This was business. I had to see Diana. In only a short period of time I grew extremely close to her. If everything went well, she had the potential to be my soulmate. I had to get this right.

The pictures at her home proved she was real, so now I just needed to connect the dots. I couldn't explain half the things that ran through my mind but seeing her in the flesh would be a good first step toward calming some of my worries.

As the clock inched toward 5:15 p.m., I had already thought about just about every possible thing that could go wrong. There were potential issues and pitfalls everywhere. But there simply wasn't enough time to solve them.

The best thing I could do was keep everything simple. I had to keep our interaction as short as possible. The longer our conversation went the more likely it was that something would go terribly wrong. I had to avoid doing a lot of talking.

I needed to just say hello and then tell her why I stopped by and then I had to be out. I was only there for confirmation. Nothing else.

I wasn't there to ask her a ton of questions. Asking her a bunch of questions could lead to her asking me a bunch of questions and I didn't want that. I had to keep the conversation short. Anything else could be disastrous.

I had to make sure things went smoothly. If they didn't, I could only imagine the bizarre headlines. Crazed man drives seven hours to meet a woman he says he met in his dream. Man, then breaks into the woman's home and snoops around and takes pictures of her personal belongings. Then the crazed man shows up at the library to stalk her and her young son.

As a writer I could certainly picture a story like that. And just about every part of it was true. Everything except the part about me stalking her. In my mind I wasn't doing that. I was just trying to find proof that she existed.

I was following my heart and doing what any other man in my situation would do. I couldn't think of one single person who had ever woken from a powerful dream and didn't wish it was real; wish it was more than just a dream. Well, I was making sure my dream came true and I was determined to not let mine slip away.

And so far, with a few exceptions everything was going right. My instincts were on point, and I was determined to see this thing through. It was now 5:15 p.m. and time for me to head to the library.

It was a short drive away and located in the back of a busy shopping plaza. With the clock ticking it was time for me to make my move. When I got to the library, I parked in the rear of the parking lot far away from the entrance.

I didn't wanna be seen so I knew a space in the back was a good place to park. I sat in my car for ten minutes and then at 5:30 I made my way inside the library.

I was nervous and each step I took toward the entrance seemed to take longer than the last. As I got

111

close, I tried to channel my anxiety into something else. Instead of being nervous I tried to sike myself into feeling like I was excited.

Like the excitement someone would have if they were going to meet an old friend they hadn't seen in a long time. As I walked through the parking lot I tried as best I could to imitate the emotions I would feel when I saw her. But as much as I tried, I just couldn't.

This was something I couldn't rehearse. I needed to be cool and just go with the flow. When I opened the library doors, I was ready and calm and mentally prepared. But then my anxiety came back when I realized I hadn't planned how I would interact with her son.

Other than his name, which was Isaac, I didn't know much about him. If he said hello to me, what would I say back? How would I conversate with him? I reminded myself to keep everything simple. I would just say hello back, then wave at him and say, "Hey what's up little man."

That was all the conversation he would get from me. I had to avoid him as much as possible. My focus was on his mother. She was the only reason I was there.

As I cleared my head and walked through the library I was surprised by how big and nice it was. In the middle of the library were rows and rows of small workstations and each one had its own computer. On the sides of the library were isles and isles of books.

In the rear of the library were several medium-sized tables and each one seemed to have someone sitting there doing work. Some people were reading books, while others were sitting down listening to music. This was a nice facility.

When I reached the rear of the library, I instinctively took a quick left. I don't know why I turned left instead of right, but my initial instincts paid off. As soon as I turned left, I saw her.

She was sitting at a table scrolling through her phone while her son sat next to her. He had a book in his hands with headphones on and he was preoccupied with the book he was reading. As I walked toward Diana, I didn't have time to make any adjustments. I had to act normal.

I was walking right toward her. Everything was happening fast. When Diana looked up and turned her head in my direction our eyes immediately locked onto each other. When she saw me, she stood up, smiled and walked toward me. She was excited and clearly thought I was the man in the pictures at her home.

She walked up to me and gave me a hug and started our conversation.

"Hey… man. What are you doing here? I thought you were going out of town. I got your card and that was so nice. But what are you doing here?"

At this point her son (who had headphones on and was preoccupied with the book he was reading) waved at me and said hello. I waved back at him then started my conversation with his mother. I was glad that was the only interaction he needed from me.

I told her, "I just stopped by to see you before I left… or should I say before I left again."

She said, "What do you mean, left again?"

I said, "I got all the way there. Went all the way to Jefferson County and forgot to bring my social security card. They need two forms of ID, and I left mine in my dresser drawer. So, I had to drive back here to get it."

"Oh… okay. Well, why didn't you just call me? You didn't have to swing by," she said.

Then I said, "I wanted to, but I left my phone at the courthouse. I left it as collateral. I offered to leave my phone

113

so they knew I was coming back. I didn't have all my ID and they were gonna scratch me from the jury.

"But when I offered to leave my phone, they said they would allow me to check in late. As long as I'm back before 8.00 p.m. I'm good. So, I can't stay long. I just stopped by to see you before I left."

Then Diana said, "Well that was nice of you. I'm glad you swung by. I'm gonna miss talking to you while you're gone. I hate that we can't talk to each other. That's a long time. You're gonna be gone for almost two weeks."

I replied, "Yeah, I know. That's why I wanted to swing by. Just to see you before I left."

Diana countered, "Well that was awfully sweet of you. You're such a nice man but you need to get going. I would hate for you to be late. And you don't know what the traffic is gonna be like."

I agreed with her and said, "Yeah, I guess I should get going."

Then she concluded, "Yes you should. And you be safe on the road. And thanks again for stopping by."

And that was it. After our conversation Diana gave me another hug and then waved me goodbye. As I walked away from her, I turned back and waved at her and her son. And then... that was it. That was my confirmation.

I had confirmed exactly what I needed to. I had proven that Diana was real, that she lived on Blue Heart Lane and that she was as beautiful in person as she was in my dream. I was grateful to know I had not made all this up. That this was not a beautiful dream. Diana was real. Very real.

Now all I had to do was figure out how to put this mysterious puzzle together.

To do that I knew I needed to make my way to Jefferson County. I had to find out who the mysterious man was in the pictures at her house. I needed to get as much information about him as possible.

There was so much I didn't know. I needed answers. At this point tons of questions were running through my head. Like why me and the man at her house looked so much alike.

We looked so much alike that Diana couldn't tell us apart. The whole time she talked to me she thought I was him. And as relieved as I was that she didn't have any suspicions about me, everything that just happened was strange. It was an uncomfortably weird and awkward experience.

Diana welcomed me. She embraced me. She told me she would miss me while I was gone. I was completely energized but I knew I had to figure out who the man in the pictures was. I knew she didn't miss me. She missed him.

I needed to know more about him to get closer to her. This was not gonna be an easy task. But if I could figure this out, Diana would be mine for the taking. She wasn't just a woman from my dream, she was the woman *of* my dreams.

She was the most beautiful woman I had ever come in contact with. I had to figure this out. There was too much at stake. I needed to solve this puzzle. And solving it was exactly what I planned to do.

Chapter 17

The Colombian

My next step was to make my way to Jefferson County. That was where I could get the answers I needed. The man in the pictures was there and he held the key to solving this puzzle. I needed to see him.

I had to find out who he was and what role he played in Diana's life. He was in my way. He and he alone stood in the way of my destiny. My future soulmate.

I had a lot of questions for him. But what would I do when I came face to face with him? I knew I couldn't explain why we looked so much alike but that was the least of my problems. How could I explain to him that I had fallen in love with a woman he seemingly was in a relationship with?

How could I explain that I had traveled over seven hours to see *his* woman? That I broke into his woman's home and snooped and took pictures and even read her mail?

There were so many things I couldn't explain. But when I hit the road for my two-hour drive to Jefferson County, I knew things would work themselves out. They always did.

And as much as I wanted to speed things up, I had to slow things down. I couldn't rush this. Solving this puzzle was going to take time and I needed to be patient and precise. As I traveled up the interstate, I realized that I also needed to define my intentions.

I had to be clear to myself of what it was that I was trying to accomplish. What was it that I was planning to do? Unfortunately, I didn't know. I didn't know what I planned to do, say or how I intended to feel when I got to Jefferson County. The only thing I knew was that Jefferson County was my next stop, and if everything went as I hoped, I would be one step closer to Diana.

The man in the pictures was set to be a juror on a big case in Jefferson County. I knew the chances of me being able to talk to him would be slim, but I had to find a way to get close to him. The note he left for Diana said the trial was scheduled to last for two weeks so I knew that was all the time I had. I had two weeks to solve this puzzle. Now the only thing I needed was a plan.

I had to figure out how long I would stay in Jefferson County. Would I stay for the whole two weeks of the trial, and if so, what would I do for the two weeks I was there? That was a long time to be in an unfamiliar place with nothing to do.

I needed to get a hotel room. I needed to call my job and request time off. I needed to get clothes.

I needed to do a lot of things, but most importantly I needed a plan. So far, the only plan I had was to be patient. I had to take my time and see how this thing goes. I had traveled too far and there was no turning back.

When I arrived in Jefferson County, I found an affordable hotel about twenty minutes from the courthouse. It was close enough that I could get to the courthouse quickly but far enough that I would have time to process my thoughts on my drive back to the hotel. The hotel I found was nothing to write home about, but it was cozy, clean and convenient.

After I checked in, I went to my room and laid down on my bed with my head resting on a pillow. It felt good to

117

be here. With a place to relax and rest it was easier for me to contemplate my next steps.

I was anxious and couldn't wait for tomorrow to get here. That was the first day of the trial. That would be my first opportunity to see the man from the pictures.

I was curious to see him, but I wasn't sure how that would work. I knew I couldn't just show up at the courthouse as myself. The man in the jury might notice me and that would complicate things.

Seeing a person who looked exactly like you sitting only a few feet away would be a major distraction. I needed to be in disguise. I had to blend in. I needed to look like just another courtroom spectator.

So I got up from my bed and headed to do a little shopping. The first stop I made was to the local mall. While there I picked up a week's worth of clothes and other things I needed for my stay. At one store I bought several polo shirts, a couple of pairs of slacks and a pair of dress shoes. And then at another store I stumbled on several items I needed for my disguise.

I bought a fake mustache, a pair of clear eyeglasses and a small two-inch afro wig, just the things I needed to conceal my identity. After gathering these things, I headed back to my hotel room and tried everything on.

The mustache, eyeglasses and wig all did as intended. They concealed my appearance. I was physically ready for tomorrow. The next thing I needed to do was drive by the courthouse to become familiar with the route I would take to get there. I needed to get a feel for the traffic in the area and see what the parking options around the courthouse were.

I wanted to avoid any type of road construction or issues along my route that could slow me down and make me late for the trial. I had to find out what time the courthouse opened and what time they allowed spectators. I also needed to know how many spectators they allowed inside each day for the trial.

This was a really small town, so I pictured the courthouse as being a small building. So small that I imagined I would need to get there early in the morning to assure I have a parking space. I wanted to find a parking space close to the courthouse.

In my mind I pictured the place having a small parking lot that was sure to be filled to the brim with cars. I might have to walk quite a way for parking. I figured I might need to leave extra early in the morning to prepare for parking issues.

But as I drove closer to the courthouse, I noticed things were not at all like I had envisioned. This was in fact a small town, but the courthouse was anything but small. It was just the opposite. The courthouse was huge and the area around it had enough parking to accommodate hundreds of people.

I was blown away by what I saw. It was late in the evening, it was almost 8 p.m. and the whole area around the courthouse was packed with people standing around talking.

There were police cars and news trucks, dog walkers and food trucks. There were people out everywhere. The scene around the courthouse was unbelievable. My first thought was that there must have been a shooting or some type of major incident in the area.

I couldn't understand why all these people were there. It was late in the evening and people were standing around like they were enjoying a festival or sorts. But this wasn't a block party. I learned right away that the people were there because of the trial that was set to take place.

As I got closer to the courthouse, I could see the reporters were broadcasting live. They were broadcasting from all around the courthouse lawn. The place was electric and something big was brewing.

The courthouse itself was absolutely beautiful. It was a large, newly constructed building that seemed much too grandiose for this small town. It wasn't just a courthouse; it was a federal courthouse.

A large breathtaking structure that represented the seventh federal district, this place was built for big cases, and the one set for tomorrow was clearly just what it was built for. I was caught up in the moment and my curiosity made me hurry to find a parking space.

I couldn't wait to get the scoop on what was going on. As soon as I parked and stepped out of my car, I walked to the first reporter I saw and asked him why there were so many people here. I asked him what was going on inside the courthouse.

He told me there was a major trial that was set to start tomorrow. The man on trial was Julius Cordova. He said the man was a well-known Colombian drug lord who had been targeted by the United States for the past ten years. He said the man allegedly ran a well-organized drug ring that funneled drugs all along the eastern seaboard, from Boston all the way down I-95 to Miami.

As a reporter and journalist, I was very familiar with Mr. Cordova. I had read about him and knew a great deal about his story. He was a well-known target of the FBI.

He was even dubbed as Mr. Untouchable because the government could never lock him up on charges. I remember the man from the pictures at Diana's house wrote a message on the card saying he was to be a juror in Jefferson County on a big case, but never in my wildest dreams would I have imagined he would be a juror on *this* case.

This was a federal case and a really big one. I wondered why the government decided to hold it in this small town. Most people would figure it would have been tried in Atlanta, DC, New York, or some other major city. But from what I heard they chose this place because the courthouse was well designed and easy to secure.

The police had the whole perimeter closed off and that would have been an almost impossible task in a large urban city. Julius Cordova was a ruthless businessman. He was involved in everything from drugs, murder, extorsion and fraud.

And the government had what many considered an airtight case against him. They had years of wire taps, surveillance videos, eyewitness testimonies and a slew of other documents proving his guilt. Everyone knew about this guy.

He was involved in just about every type of criminal activity there was. But there was one thing that made him notorious. It was the one crime that many people consider the most egregious act a person could commit.
Mr. Cordova was one of the largest human traffickers in North America.

He trafficked young, teenage girls from all over Central and South America. His organization would bring girls to the United States and Canada and sell them to the wealthiest of businesspeople. He called his girls the International A-Team and people paid hundreds of thousands of dollars to exploit them.

His said clientele involved only the wealthiest of Americans and Canadians. Supposedly businesspeople, lawyers, doctors, entertainers, and all types of people with big money to spend. There were also alleged state politicians, foreign nationals and even higher up members of the United States government involved in his criminal enterprise.

In the eyes of the law Mr. Cordova was a wanted man. But what made him "Mr. Untouchable" was his claim to have videos and recordings of several members of Congress, top government agents and even white house officials, all allegedly engaged in sexual relations with his young victims. Out of fear of being exposed, these higher up officials would reach down to local law enforcement agents and instruct them to turn a blind eye to Cordova's criminal activities.

He had protection from everywhere. No one could or would ever attempt to arrest him. He was too dangerous. He had so much political power that local authorities had to get permission to question him or any member of his criminal enterprise.

Federal prosecutors and district attorneys all turned a blind eye. Not one of them ever brought charges against him. Law enforcement agencies from all the way up in Boston and all the way down in Miami all went silent. Not one of them ever went after him.

Over the years several members of his organization were killed, arrested, or prosecuted for crimes they committed while working for him, but *he* seemingly went untouched. And now after nearly a decade of being Mr. Untouchable, he was finally being brought to justice. This was a really big case.

No one knew what to expect. No one knew why the government decided that now was the time to hold him accountable. What information did they have now that they didn't have years ago? Those questions fueled everyone's interest and that was the reason why everyone tuned in to this case.

Now I understood why there was such a heavy police presence around the courthouse. The security had to be tight. This was the biggest criminal case in the United States in over half a century. And because of its importance, the reporter said assassination rumors were running rampant.

He said there were alleged to be privately hired snipers who had blended with the crowd and were tasked with killing Mr. Cordova. They were given a green light to shoot and kill him at the first chance they got.

There were also reports of witness tampering, bribery, and tons of threats to kill witnesses to prevent testimony. It was clear that a lot of people wanted to keep Mr. Cordova from talking and they desperately wanted to keep his video recordings from going public. Videos and recordings that were said to expose corrupt politicians and had the potential to rock the United States political world at its core.

But in spite of the government claiming to have over a thousand hours of video evidence, confidential documents and witness testimony directly implicating him, not many people believed this case would ever make it to a jury. There was too much at stake. If the evidence and information he claimed to have been true, the people he implicated would do anything in their power to make sure the case never made it to trial.

Even if that meant trying to kill the most powerful drug dealer and criminal mastermind in the Western Hemisphere. For what it was worth, Mr. Cordova always declared his innocence. He repeatedly said he was the target of a government smear campaign and vowed revenge on anyone who tried to cross him.

And when a man of his status issued a threat, people certainly took him seriously. Earlier in the year while on a Spanish radio station he told callers that he had dirt on one U.S. governor, three U.S. senators and even a high-ranking member of the white house administration. All secretly recorded on hidden audio and video engaged in inappropriate sexual activities with his underaged girls.

He threatened that if any charges were ever brought against him, he would expose American politics at its core. Then, showing no fear of prosecution, he gave a phone number to all of his radio listeners and encouraged them to call and place an order for the services of the young women of his so-called International A-Team.

He told his listeners that as long as he had videos of crooked politicians, it was safe to do business with him. Mr. Cordova was a confident, arrogant, and extremely dangerous businessman. It was about time the government finally stood up and did the right thing. No man is supposed to be above the law and now that famous creed was being put to the test.

Because of the nature of this trial his bail had been denied. Mr. Cordova was sure to leave the country if given the opportunity and the government vowed not to let that happen. For his safety Mr. Cordova was escorted to court by armed federal FBI agents. He was ordered to wear a bulletproof vest and was to be shielded by a bulletproof shield whenever he exited the courtroom.

The government was committed to keeping him safe. Even if it meant risking the lives of everyone around him. They were determined to bring him to justice.

After walking around the courthouse and taking in all the excitement, it was already late, so I decided to head back to my hotel to rest up and get ready for the next day. I was glad it was only a short twenty-minute drive away. I was tired and I looked forward to getting some much-needed rest.

The next morning when I awoke, I felt a sense of eagerness that I hadn't felt in a long time. As I gathered my things and prepared for my drive to the courthouse, I knew today would be a special day. I couldn't help but think how this felt eerily similar to the feeling I had when I met Diana at the library.

Just like then, I was nervous, but I was also extremely calm and ready to get the ball rolling. As I picked out my clothes, I put on a pair of black dress slacks and a white polo shirt. I didn't want to be overdressed by wearing a tie and I didn't want to be underdressed by wearing jeans and sneakers. I needed to be comfortable, and I needed to blend in.

After I got dressed, I took out a tube of glue and placed a thin layer of it on my top lip. This was the glue that would be used to hold my fake mustache in place. It was really easy to use and looked like a tube of ChapStick. I would bring this with me in case the glue on my lip wore off during the day.

I also had a pair of clear, black-framed glasses, and when I put them on, they added to concealing my identity. Next, I placed the half inch black afro on my head. When I looked in the mirror I looked like a completely different person. With my identity officially concealed I was ready to head to the courthouse.

As I walked out of my hotel room it was 6:00 a.m. The hotel parking lot was quiet, and I was the only person moving around at this time of morning. When I started my car, I turned on the radio and listened to some easy music for my short drive to the courthouse.

When I arrived at the courthouse, just like yesterday, there were reporters hovering across the lawn preparing for their early morning broadcasts. I parked across the street from the courthouse and walked past at least three news networks, one of which was already doing a live broadcast. The other two were preparing to go live and were working out their early morning kinks.

As I approached the entrance to the courthouse there was already a small line of people waiting to be spectators at the trial. Standing in front of me were about five or six people. And shortly after I stepped in line another four or five people lined up behind me. As the clock ticked and time passed, the line behind me swelled and stretched nearly all the way along the side and to the rear of the building. There were a lot of people who wanted to be spectators in this trial.

When I glanced around, I noticed that most of the people in line appeared to be journalists and reporters. They were either on their phones talking about the case or writing down notes on their notepads. Outside of myself there weren't many people I would consider ordinary.

After all, most ordinary people wouldn't stand in line at 6:30 a.m. to witness a court trial. As the time passed the sun began to rise and the crowd around the courthouse continued to swell.

By now there were at least a hundred people out. Either standing around, standing on the lawn around the courthouse or waiting in line to be a spectator. And as the morning inched along, I started to see more and more ordinary people like myself coming out.

Small groups of local people popped up and could be seen standing around talking. Some stood in the shade while others stood in line at food trucks and talked to people standing near them. Everyone was getting in on the action.

Every hour the size of the crowd grew, and I was anxious to see the inside of the courthouse. This trial was probably the largest event to happen in this town in its entire history and the townspeople knew it. This was a *big* case.

It involved a man who openly defied and broke the law and threatened anyone who got in his way. And it was those threats that made this the most bizarre and entertaining case in the country. Every good-willed American would eventually tune into this trial with the hope that Mr. Cordova might release videos of the alleged crooked politicians.

And the list of politicians who people speculated would be implicated in this case grew by the day. There was even a website that allowed people to cast bets on which politicians they thought would be implicated. People placed all kinds of bets on who they thought would be exposed.

And for lawmakers and politicians, having their names appear on these betting websites was not good. Being tied to a "Most Likely to Go to Jail" website was definitely bad for reelection. They wanted this trial over before it even started.

After waiting in line for what seemed like forever, a trial clerk came out and told us that the court would be in session soon. I looked at my watch and it was just past 7:30, I had been standing in line for almost an hour. Like everybody else I was ready to go inside. I looked forward to sitting down and resting and I hoped the seats weren't hard benches like the kinds in most courthouses.

Then finally at 8:00 a.m. we slowly filed into the courtroom. We went through a series of metal detectors and then were escorted to courtroom number five. There were other cases in other courtrooms happening at the same time as ours and people were coming and going and moving in all different directions.

As I walked into the courtroom, I was ushered to a seat on the far left of the pews. The benches we sat on were hard, but it felt good to finally have a seat anyway, and my seat was a good one.

From where I sat, I could clearly see all the members of the jury and I was so close that I could probably hear their conversations when they spoke to each other.

As the courtroom continued to fill, I felt the magnitude of the trial. I couldn't believe I was here.

Not only would I have a front row seat to observe a man who looked eerily similar to me, but I was sitting in a courtroom where the jury would have the enormous task of determining the guilt or innocence of a powerful international crime boss. As the jury entered, my heart raced and beat hard like a drum. I was excited.

As a journalist, this was what we dreamed of. This was going to be a magnificent story, worthy of me taking notes and writing about it every day. But I wasn't focused on the trial.

That's not why I was here. I was focused on the man I had traveled here to see. And I didn't have to wait long to see what I had come for.

Chapter 18

J3

When the jury was escorted into the courtroom my eyes instantly locked in on him. He was the third juror to enter the courtroom and he sat in the third seat farthest from left. He sat in the seat assigned for juror number three.

When he sat down, he did the same thing all the other jurors did. He turned his head from left to right and scanned the courtroom. This was their moment to take everything in.

The courtroom was packed with reporters, police officers, spectators and cameras pointing in all directions. As he looked around and scanned the courtroom, I made sure not to catch eyes with him. When he looked in my direction I turned and looked away.

And when he looked away, I stared at him. I couldn't take my eyes off him. He actually looked just like me. He had all my features and appeared to be the same height, weight, body type and complexion as me. Everything about us was similar. No matter how hard I tried I couldn't make sense of it.

And I watched him like he was on display. I watched how he interacted with the jurors around him. I watched how he held his pen and took notes. I watched how often he glanced around the courtroom. I even took notice of whether or not he was engaged or disengaged. I watched him like a hawk.

I had traveled all this way to see him and there he was, only a few feet away from me. I wanted to hear his voice. I wanted to talk to him and ask him questions. But for now, none of that was possible. All I could do was watch.

Watch him and wait for my opportunity. Sitting there in the courtroom I had no idea how this would play out, but I was glad to be here. Minutes later, when everyone finally packed into the courtroom, the judge gave his orders that everyone was to remain quiet at all times. He said there were to be no distractions, unnecessary movements or outbursts of any kind during the trial.

He then pointed to the sheriff's deputies stationed around and instructed them to arrest anyone in the courtroom who didn't follow his orders. When he spoke the tension in the room was thick. It was so quiet you could hear a pin drop.

As the trial began, I noticed that the members of the jury were only identified by their numbers. There was juror number one who was seated closest to me and juror number twelve who was seated the furthest away. The man I had traveled here to see was juror number three. And since I didn't know his name, I decided that's what I would call him. I called him J3. That was the name I gave him until I could find his real identity.

And then there was Mr. Cordova. When he entered the courtroom, he was emotionless and didn't say a word. He sat next to his team of high-priced lawyers and silently looked on. And although he was seated directly in front of me, he was the furthest thing from my mind.

I hardly paid any attention to him. I wasn't there for him. I was there for J3. He was the only person that had my absolute full attention.

The first day of trial was nothing spectacular. Even if I had been paying attention there was nothing to write about.

Mostly procedural stuff. Nothing major, no new news. Just motions and motions and then more motions.

The lawyers were arguing over what evidence would be allowed and which witnesses would testify, and which ones wouldn't. And after that they discussed policies and procedures and then they went back to discussing motions and motions and more motions.

After the first day my head was spinning. I was bored and ready for day one to be over. At the conclusion of day one I left the courthouse, walked back to my car, and sat down on the driver seat to process everything that had happened today. I felt relieved that I had the opportunity to finally see J3, but I felt cheated knowing I hadn't accomplished anything.

I wondered what I was going to do tomorrow. I didn't know what the future held but I knew at some point I needed a plan. I just didn't have one yet. I knew I needed information on J3 but for now I didn't see how that was possible.

But I was confident that everything would work itself out. I just needed to be patient and take this one day at a time. Before I drove back to my hotel I decided to stop and get a quick bite to eat.

Early this morning I saw there was a waffle house across the street from my hotel so after I parked my car, I took off my fake mustache and my small afro wig and went inside for a quick bite to eat. I didn't stay very long. Just long enough to woof down a burger and fries and a large strawberry milkshake.

The food and service at the restaurant were both good so I figured this would be my new dining spot after the long days in court. I hadn't eaten all day at the courthouse, so I wasn't sure if the food was really good or if I was simply starving, but that was the best burger I had eaten in a long time. After I ate my meal, I headed back to my hotel where I laid down and crashed.

The next thing I remembered was waking up the next morning. The next day I got up early like I had done the day before. I ironed a pair of dark brown khakis and a white polo shirt. Then I stood in the mirror and placed my mustache over my lip, threw on my small afro wig then placed my clear glasses in my shirt pocket. I was ready to make my twenty-minute drive to the courthouse.

I arrived at the courthouse at 6:30 a.m. just as I had yesterday. And once again there were news trucks stationed all along the lawn in front of the massive federal building. The crowd outside was about the same size as the day before and everything seemed to be going smoothly. However, one thing was noticeably different.

The line of spectators had grown. It had grown significantly. Yesterday at this same time I was fifth in line but today, I was much, much further back. There were a lot more people in the line.

I knew tomorrow I needed to get here a little earlier. Yesterday I had a good seat and today I was just hoping to get in. There had to be at least fifteen to twenty people in front of me and that wasn't good. I didn't travel all this way to stand outside all day. I needed to be in the courtroom.

Tomorrow, I had to leave the hotel earlier. I couldn't risk this happening again.

Fortunately, everything worked out for me and at 8:00 a.m. we filed into the courthouse just as we had done the day before. And right after we sat down the jurors made their way to their seats J3 was third in line again and sat in his usual seat.

And oddly enough, today he was dressed very similarly to me. I had on dark brown khaki pants and a white polo shirt, and he had on dark brown khaki pants and

132

white polo shirt. As strange as that was, I didn't read that much into it.

Most of the male jurors had polo shirts too. The only real coincidence was that we had the same color and similar type pants. This man not only looked like me but now he appeared to be dressed like me too. I was a little puzzled, but I took it as a coincidence.

It wasn't something I was gonna spend a great deal of my time thinking about. I had other things on my mind that were more important than how he dressed. The second day of trial started just like it ended yesterday. There was evidence and more evidence and then testimony and more testimony. I wasn't interested in the trail at all. I spent most of my time in court watching J3. I was consumed by him. I watched his every move.

I tried not to stare at him but at times I found it fascinating that this man looked so much like me. As he sat there, I studied his every move. I was analyzing him to help me solve the mystery of who he was. I was sure witnesses and testimonies going on in the trial were interesting, but all my interests were on J3.

Throughout the second day J3 seemed to be very interested in the court proceedings. He was taking notes and seemed very attentive. But at one point during the second day his attention began to drift. He appeared to be losing interest and started looking around at different people in the courtroom.

At one point I think he was focused on me. I didn't want to catch eyes with him so I looked away, but I could feel him looking at me. And a few seconds later I looked back at him and sure enough he was still looking and seemingly staring at me.

It made me very uncomfortable, so I looked away again. And this time I didn't look back at him for a long time.

It had to be like thirty minutes. And not looking at him for that long was difficult.

I had been focused on him all day for the past two days. And as much as I wanted to look at him, I couldn't risk it. If he saw me staring at him, he might sense something was up and that would not be good. So, I looked away and focused on the trial.

Up to this moment I hadn't been paying attention to anything and I didn't know what was going on. But for the rest of the day, I kept my eyes off him. I listened to witness testimonies and patiently waited for this day to end. After the second day of trial came to an end, I did the same thing I had done the day before.

I left the courthouse, got in my car, and headed back to the waffle house for a bite to eat. When I pulled into the parking lot, I took off my wig and fake mustache and went inside. Only this time instead of a greasy burger I ordered something a little healthier. I ordered two grilled pork chops, macaroni and cheese and a glass of sweet tea.

After I ate, I went back to my room and tried to prepare myself for the next day of trial. When I was back in my room, I laid back my head on my pillow and thought about the past three days I had spent in this town. That's when I realized I hadn't done anything.

The whole time I had been in this small town I hadn't accomplished a single thing. It was a frustrating reality check. I came here to get answers about J3 but three days later I wasn't any closer to solving who he was than when I first got here. I was only a few feet away from him, but I had no opportunity to speak with him or interact with him at all.

I felt like I was wasting my time and I started second guessing myself about my trip here. I realized I might never get to speak to J3. Aside from other jurors, he wasn't allowed to speak to anyone in the courtroom. How in the world could I ask questions to someone I never got the chance to talk to?

Maybe I could slip a note to him that had a bunch of questions written on it. That sounded like a good plan. I just needed a way to get the note to him. But when I thought about it, that task was even more difficult than trying to speak with him. There was no way for me to pass him a note.

There were too many people watching and TV cameras were everywhere. If I got caught passing a note to a juror, the judge was sure to have me arrested. So, my note passing plan was over before I even had a chance to write it down on paper.

I knew I needed to do something; I just didn't know what. And I needed more time. Tomorrow was Saturday. It was the third day of a trial that was supposed to last for two weeks, and the clock was ticking.

I had to figure something out and I hoped tomorrow would provide me with answers. I needed tomorrow to be a productive day. As I prepared myself for bed all I could think about was what tomorrow would bring.

Over the past two days I hadn't accomplished anything. Tomorrow had to be different. Deep down inside I knew things would work out. I just had to be patient and stay ready for my opportunity.

The next morning, I got up, got dressed and headed to the courthouse driving the same route I had taken the past two days. Traffic was normal and my commute was no different than before. I left thirty minutes earlier today and when I arrived at the courthouse, I was the fourth person in the spectator's line.

As time passed the line behind me grew and stretched all the way around the side of the building. Today was Saturday. It was the weekend. And even though it was early in the morning there were already more people out here today than had been the past two days.

As usual, at 8:00 a.m. we were ushered into the courtroom. I was anxious to see the jury enter the courtroom so I could see how J3 was dressed. Yesterday he was dressed very similarly to me so today I was curious to see how he dressed. I didn't have to wait long because when J3 entered, once again, he was dressed like I was.

We both had on the same type of blue dress pants and a white polo shirt. For two days in a row our style of clothing was as similar as our appearance. I needed to find out who this guy was. There were so many things about him that continued to puzzle me.

Aside from his dress, everything seemed to be following the same routine. The jurors quietly entered the courtroom then took their assigned seats as they had done the past two days. Everything appeared normal but then something stood out to me. The juror seated next to J3 seemed to have an interest in him.

After they both took their seats, she leaned over and grabbed his hand, briefly rubbed it then smiled at him. It was only a few seconds of interaction, but I noticed the whole thing. When she rubbed his hand J3 began to blush and smile.

I don't know what was going on between them, but they clearly had some type of interaction that extended beyond being jurors. Something must have happened between yesterday and today. Perhaps something happened last night. The jurors were sequestered together at a hotel.

Maybe they had a few drinks at the hotel bar and made a connection. I wasn't sure. But in that short few seconds of her rubbing his hand it sure seemed like some type of connection had been made. And throughout the day this subtle nonchalant connection between the two of them became more and more noticeable.

As someone who studied and stalked J3 in the courtroom, I knew something was going on. Every time she looked at him, she blushed and smiled, and he blushed and smiled back. I couldn't believe what I was seeing. They were casually and openly flirting.

At one point I even observed them passing notes back and forth to each other.

Here they were on the third day of trial and both of their minds were clearly somewhere else. They weren't focused on Mr. Cordova or the plethora of witnesses parading in and out of the courtroom, they were focused on each other.

And as much as they tried to hide it, it was clear to me and anyone else who paid attention that there was something extra going on. The smiling, smirking, hand patting and hand rubbing continued throughout the day and began to bother me.

It actually angered me. My feelings towards J3 began to change. Every time I looked at him my face filled with disgust. He had a beautiful woman at home and here he was flirting with a woman who clearly was of no comparison to Diana.

I had no ill feelings toward the woman because I was sure she had no idea about Diana or J3's relationship with her. The woman appeared to be friendly and outgoing. She was a pretty, young Hispanic woman who I'm sure was a pleasure to be seated next to. But watching them smile and flirt with each other all day was difficult for me.

I cared deeply for Diana, but she was out of my reach. And to see the one person who stood in my way acting like he had no care in the world about her, that really frustrated me. It made me dislike and despise him even more.

Throughout the day I did nothing but watch. I was powerless to do anything else. And at the end of the day when I walked to my car, I felt like I had reached my boiling point with J3. When this trial was over, I planned to confront him.

I was gonna tell him he didn't deserve Diana and tell him I saw him flirting with the young juror seated next to him. I would tell him how I felt about Diana and that I would do everything I could to be with her. I planned to give him a piece of my mind.

As I drove back to my hotel all I could think about was how J3 was betraying Diana. He didn't care about her. Not like I did. I had to tell him how I felt.

Later that night as I laid on my bed thinking, I realized my plan was based on emotions rather than logic. As much as I wanted to confront J3 I was in no position to do so. After three days of trial, I still didn't know much about him. I still didn't know his name.

But I did feel like I was figuring him out. The gains I was making were small, but I knew I was making progress. I had to be patient and stay the course. I felt like the tiny pieces of this massive puzzle were finally starting to come together. I figured tomorrow would be special.

The fourth day of trial started early Sunday morning. I had hoped something different might happen today. That more pieces of this puzzle would take shape. Yesterday I learned that J3 was not all that he appeared to be. He didn't love Diana. He was an imposter and at the end of the trial I planned to expose him.

Yesterday he and his young juror friend smiled and flirted throughout the day. And today, to my dismay, they were at it again. But today they were even more noticeable than they were the day before. They almost seemed like a couple. I can't count the number of times I saw her make eye contact with him. She couldn't keep her eyes off him.

And he couldn't keep his eyes off her. I'm sure the other jurors also talked to each other after the long days in court. I'm sure they made friendships and enjoyed each other's company. But J3 and his young friend were doing more than the average jurors. They were openly flirting with each other, and it really bothered me.

I simply couldn't believe that J3 would jeopardize his relationship with Diana for this young juror. I couldn't believe he could be so selfish. He clearly wasn't a smart man. He was foolish. And as I sat in the courtroom, I felt more and more like my role was to expose him for the fraud that he was.

I had to find a way to eliminate him. I needed to remove him from the picture. I just didn't know how. So far there hadn't been any opportunity for me to confront him, question him or do anything other than watch him. I hadn't done anything worth mentioning in the five days I'd been in this town.

After a few hours, when the trial broke for a two-hour lunch break, I sat outside on one of the benches in the courtyard and depression overtook me. I couldn't stomach watching J3 smirk and flirt with his young mistress any longer. I was depleted.

I traveled all this way, and I haven't accomplished anything. Sitting on the bench in the open courtyard I realized that this trip here was a failure. I had spent five days in this town, and I had nothing to show for it.

I couldn't speak to J3 and even if I could I had no plan for what I would tell him. My whole being here made no sense. I felt pitiful. I felt like a failure.

All I wanted was Diana. That's all I cared about. But somehow, I got dragged to this small town in the middle of nowhere and was sitting in on a trial I had zero interest in.

I had no idea what was going on in the courtroom. My only focus was on J3. He consumed me. All day, every day, I studied his every move. And after five days I realized this whole thing was a disaster.

I didn't have a plan. Nothing I was doing here made any sense. So, I decided today was my last day in this town. I was giving up.

Chapter 19

Unwelcome Guests

I wasn't going back into the courthouse after the lunch break. I was done. I admitted defeat and was headed back to my hotel room. I was disappointed because I knew I had failed.

I traveled all this way for nothing. I tried to pick my head up as I walked to my car, but I was so frustrated and weak that it was hard for me to do. It was a terrible feeling.

When I got to my car and sat in the driver seat my feelings somewhat changed. I wasn't depressed any more. I felt relieved. It felt good to be done with J3 and this whole meaningless trial.

I wasn't sure if giving up on J3 meant I was also giving up on Diana, but it felt good to know I didn't have to sit in that courtroom another day. I hated the thought of letting Diana go but I realized there was no way for me to remove J3 from the picture.

It crushed me to think about never seeing her again, but I understood that was the likely outcome of me leaving the trial. Without knowing who J3 was I had no chance of getting close to Diana. And I knew I couldn't go back to see her again.

As much as I wanted to say goodbye to her one last time, I knew that wasn't possible. She would never understand my situation. And there was no way for me to ever explain it.

And if I drove through her town one last time to see her, if she spotted me, that would make the situation worse. There would be no way I could explain how I was in two places at the same time. I had to stay away.

Tons of thoughts raced through my head. I needed to clear my thoughts, so I turned on the car radio and found a smooth jazz station. It was just what I needed. As the music played, I felt better about my situation.

And when I drove out of the courthouse parking lot, I knew this was my last day in this town. The only thing left for me to do was to check out of the hotel and hit the road again. And I was ready to go. I wanted to go home.

I was relieved that this was over. All I wanted was a nice meal before I left this town, and I knew just where to get one. My last meal would be at the Waffle House I had eaten at for the past four days. The food and service were good, and the restaurant was clean and welcoming.

So that was my plan. Eat there one last time and then check out of the hotel and hit the road. I had a long drive ahead of me. It was going to take me seven hours to get home, so a good meal was just what I needed to fuel up.

Before I left, I told my boss that I was taking some time off to visit a sick relative. When I got home, I would return to work and get back to the life I lived just a few short days ago. I was starting to feel better about things. I welcomed the thought of going home. I liked the simple life I lived and looked forward to returning to it.

As soon as I had driven away from the courthouse, I took off my wig and fake mustache and threw them both on the passenger seat. I felt good to be taking them off for the last time. It felt good seeing those items on the passenger seat instead of on my head and glued to my top lip.

With the sound of smooth jazz seeping through my speakers I arrived at the Waffle House for my last meal in this town. But when I pulled into the parking lot something strange happened. Just as I pulled in, a large SUV pulled alongside of me, and the driver motioned for me to roll down my window.

The driver was an older gentleman and he appeared to need help. As I rolled down my window to offer my assistance the man pulled out a camera and took three to four quick pictures of my face and then sped off. Before I even had a chance to say a word, he was gone.

I was startled by what just happened. I couldn't help but wonder what that was all about. Why did he do that? Did he think I was someone famous? I couldn't make sense of it. But I wasn't gonna let some wanna be paparazzi stop me from enjoying a good meal before I left town.

So I went into the restaurant and ordered two eggs, a piece of toast and a cup of coffee. As I ate, I couldn't help but think about the man in the SUV. Why did he waive my attention? Why did he speed off like he did? And why did he take pictures of me?

I didn't really know what he was doing, and I didn't really care. I was about to leave this place and the last thing on my mind was an old, demented man taking pictures of people while he was out joy riding.

He was probably crazy. That was the only explanation I could come up with and it made sense. The old man clearly was a nutcase.

As I finished my meal I got back in my car and made the twenty-minute drive to my hotel. I was a little disappointed checking out of the hotel because I was gonna lose money on the room. I had already prepaid for the room for ten nights and I was leaving after only staying five nights. I hated losing money, but I knew in this case there wasn't anything I could do about it.

After I parked, I grabbed my wig, my fake mustache, and the clear glasses from the passenger seat, placed them in my pocket then went inside my room. I didn't wanna leave them in the car. I was gonna throw them in the trash bin in my room.

When I went inside my room, I gathered my clothes, snacks, and other items I had bought for my brief stay in this small town and placed them in my suitcase. It felt good to be leaving. I hadn't accomplished what I set out to do but I felt good knowing I had given it a good try.

I was leaving here almost the same way as I arrived. Not sure of my next step but confident things would work out. I knew I had no chance of seeing Diana again, but I was okay with that. I felt a huge sense of relief that this failed experience was ending.

I didn't know what my future held but I was ready to go back to the simple life I lived five short days ago. Before I exited the room, I took the items out of my pocket and threw them all on the bed. I wasn't taking any of those with me. I was done with them.

Then I briefly looked at the items on the bed and glanced around the room. I had to take a moment to reflect on my short stay here. I told myself… you're not gonna miss this place. Nope. Not one bit.

Then I grabbed my suitcase off the floor and headed out the door. But just as I turned the door handle to exit the room a tall man with a pistol nudged me back inside. He pointed the gun at my head and told me not to make a sound. As he pushed me back in the room the door quickly closed behind him.

I immediately put my hands in the air, and I did as I was told. Once inside, he didn't say a word. He just stood there holding his gun, which was aimed directly at my face. I was terrified.

144

Within seconds he and I were engulfed in a silent stare down. I couldn't speak. I dared say a word. I was speechless, standing there with my hands up, not knowing what his motives were.

Then after what seemed an eternity, I said the only thing I could that wouldn't cause him to be alarmed. I said, "Please, please don't shoot me. I don't have anything you want. You're in the wrong room."

He didn't say a word. He just stood there holding his pistol. Then I heard a noise from behind him. It was the sound of keys. It was the sound of someone placing a key in the room door.

And then the noise briefly stopped, and the room door slowly opened. Then two more men entered my room. At this point I was even more terrified. I didn't know what was going on.

"You guys got the wrong room." I pleaded. "You got the wrong person." Then the man with the gun uttered his first words to me. He gave me a directive. He said for me not to move or attempt anything foolish and to keep my hands up if I wanted to live. And I did exactly as I was told. I nodded my head in agreement and I kept my hands up and I didn't make any unnecessary moves.

As the door closed behind the two other men, I couldn't imagine what this was about. I figured they had come to rob me, but I didn't have any money. I didn't have guns or drugs or anything they would be interested in.

The only thing I could think of was these guys were in the wrong room. They must have confused my room with someone else's. As I stood there with my hands raised, the three men began to speak quietly to one another.

I couldn't understand what they were saying, but I knew the language they were speaking was Spanish. And by their body movements I could also tell they were very

145

interested in the items I had on my bed. Not the pieces of trash and half eaten bags of chips. No. Not those items.

They were interested in the fake mustache, the wig, and the clear glasses I had thrown on the bed. They were very interested in those items. Then one of the men walked over to the bed and picked up the items. He examined them one by one.

As he held up each one the other men chimed in while speaking Spanish. After they discussed all three items, he tossed them all back on the bed. Then, after examining the items the man holding the gun lowered his weapon and placed it in a holster behind his back.

Then one of the other men spoke to me. He spoke to me in English. He told me to lower my arms and have a seat in the chair next to the bed.

I did exactly as I was told and took a seat in the chair. It was at this point that I got my first real look at all three men. Before now I was so nervous that I didn't pay attention to any of their features. The only thing I paid attention to be the gun in my face.

But once I sat down, I got a good look at all three of them. They were all Hispanic middle-aged men. All three were dressed professionally in slacks and polo shirts. And all three fit the description of a hitman you might see in an old gangster movie.

I thought for sure these guys had mistaken me for someone else when they walked into my room. I hoped they would leave peacefully when they realized I wasn't who they were looking for. I was not a criminal.

I had nothing they could be looking for. I was a law-abiding citizen, and I was hoping these guys would quickly figure that out. But after telling me to have a seat the men returned to examining the items on the bed.

All three of them just stood there hovering over the items. The room was once again silent, and I dared not make a sound. I was too scared to do anything but sit there and wait for my next order. I didn't know what they wanted, and my fear kept me from asking.

And then after what had to be at least a minute of heart pounding silence, one of the men spoke to me.

He said, "Who are you?"

I wasn't really sure what to say so I told him my name.

I said, "My name is Curtis Wilson. And I'm not who you guys are looking for. You guys got the wrong person."

Then the man said, "Shut up! I only asked you one question. When I ask one question, I only want one answer. Are we clear?"

I said, "Yes sir. Of course. I understand."

Then the man said, "Where is your wallet? Hand it to me."

I reached in my front pocket and handed him my wallet. He then went through it and pulled out my credit cards and tossed them one by one on the bed. Then he took out my driver's license, held it in the air and began asking more questions.

He said, "I'm gonna ask you again. Who are you? I don't care what this license says. I don't care about your name. I want to know who you are. Why are you here? Why are you staying at this motel? Why are you here in this place?"

At this point I was really nervous. He seemed to be interested in questions I didn't want to answer. I couldn't explain who I was. Or why I was here. Even if I wanted to tell him I didn't know how to. And even if I did tell him he wouldn't believe me. My story was a laughable fairytale. So, I tried to stall him as best I could.

I told him, "I'm not sure what you're asking me... Sir. My name is Curtis Wilson. I'm here for the trial. The big trial at the courthouse. I heard about it and wanted to

147

come checks it out for myself. I'm a journalist and I'm here for the trial."

The man replied, "You think we are stupid. You think we're gonna believe that. Why do you have these items? Why do you need these?"

The man then reached over to the bed and picked up the disguise. He then held up the wig and fake mustache while he asked a number of questions. He asked, "What journalist needs things like this? Why do you need these things?"

I told him, "Because I'm an undercover journalist. That's why I have the disguise."

Then the other man walked toward me and stopped less than a foot in front of me. He took a second to clear his throat then he joined the conversation.

He said, "That's bullshit. There is no such thing as an undercover journalist. There is no need for an undercover journalist. The press from all over the country are here. No one is in disguise but you.

"We have been watching you from the first day you arrived. We have stood in line next to you. Sometimes in front of you. Sometimes behind you. We have watched you. You are here for a reason. And it's time for you to tell us who you are."

Then the other man joined in and said, "Our time is very precious. We want to know who you are? And you better be truthful with us, or we will take the truth from you. I'm sure you know what that means.

"Either you give us the truth, or we will take it from you. We are giving you a chance to do things the easy way. I'm pretty sure you won't like the hard way."

I pleaded with the men saying, "I'm sorry but I still don't know what you're talking about. I'm a journalist. I'm not looking for any trouble."

One of the men said, "We saw you. We watched you. Every day you went to the trial. But inside the courtroom you weren't paying attention to the court. Not the witnesses, the evidence, or the testimony. Nothing. You weren't interested in any of that. You are interested in someone on the jury. One juror in particular.

"There is a man who has your interest. And now that you have taken off these disguise items, we can see that you look a lot like him. What is going on here? What are you up to?"

Suddenly I wasn't as afraid as I had been minutes earlier. I had been through a lot, and I started to feel like I didn't care. There was no way I could explain to them why I was here. I was boxed into a corner and the truth would not set me free. I wasn't telling these guys the truth. If I told them they might laugh, then kill me on the spot. So, I dug in and stuck to my story. It was the only choice I felt I had.

I said, "I told you. I'm a journalist. I'm undercover working on something. I can't tell you what it is but I'm covering this case because it's the biggest case in the country. I'm in disguise because I don't want people to know that I'm here. I wish I could tell you more, but I can't."

One of the men countered by saying, "No one puts on a disguise to go to court. No one stands in line at 6:30 in the morning to come to court and not pay any attention to what's going on. Juror number three seems to have your attention. What do you want with him? Why is he so important to you? And why do you look so much like him?"

I responded, "I wish I could tell you more but that's it. I don't know anything else. There's nothing else to tell."

Then the man asked me one more time to tell them who I was and why I was here. When I shook my head and said I didn't know what they were talking about, one of the men said it was time to go to plan B. He asked me if I knew

149

what plan B was and when I said no, he went on to explain it.

Chapter 20

Masterplan

He said, "Since you are refusing to tell us what we need to know. Now it's time for plan B. I'm sure you have watched plenty of movies. What do you think our plan B is?"

I said, "You rough me up. You guys are gonna beat me up. Torture me. I hope that's not what you're planning to do because I haven't done anything. I don't know what you want from me."

After I said that all three men turned and looked at each other then began to laugh.

They said, "Do we look like the type to roughen you up? To torture you. Do we look like the type of people to do those things? We are businessmen. That's not how we work."

So, I asked, "Well what's plan B then? What are your plans?"

Then the room got very quiet as one of the men reached behind his back and pulled out a large manila folder. Inside the folder were several pictures. He pulled the first one out and asked me if I knew who was in the picture.

When I looked at the picture, I knew exactly who it was. It was a picture of me. It was a picture of me driving my car through the Waffle House parking lot. It was one of the pictures the old man had taken of me. The old man that I thought was crazy.

I said, "Yes. I know who that is. That's me. Someone took that picture of me today while I was driving."

He then reached into the folder and pulled out another picture. It was a picture of J3.

He said, "Do you know who this is?"

I said, "Yes, that looks like one of the jurors."

Then the man paused, nodded his head, and sarcastically told me I was doing a very good job.

He said, "You are doing a good job. I'm glad you like these pictures. Plan B is going very well for you. I have a few more pictures to show you."

He then reached in the folder and took out another picture. Then he asked me the same question. If I recognized the person in the picture. I paused when I saw the picture. I couldn't answer him. I wouldn't answer him. I refused to answer him. He showed me a picture of Diana.

He said, "Oh. So, you're not going to talk? I thought you were playing the game so well. Plan B was going so smoothly. But we aren't done yet. I have more pictures for you."

He then pulled yet another picture from the folder. This time it was a picture of Diana's son.

He said, "Do you know this boy? Do you know his mother? You have been quiet for a while now. You are making this much too difficult. Just answer the questions. Do you know these people?"

I still didn't answer. I tried to look away. But he continued with his questions.

He said, "So we are almost done. I only have a few more pictures for you."

He then reached into the folder and pulled out yet another picture. He asked me again if I knew the person in the photo. This time I couldn't remain silent. The picture he showed me made me afraid. It was a picture of a dead woman and teenage boy. Their bodies were lying on the ground and were riddled with bullets. They both had been executed; shot dead.

The woman was lying on the ground and next to her was her dead son. The boy looked no more than twelve or thirteen years old and the picture of him and his mother was horrific. But that wasn't what made me afraid. What scared me was when the man asked me to take a closer look at the picture.

He said, "Now take a closer look at this picture. You may not know the woman and the boy, but do you know the people in the background? Take a closer look."

When I took a closer look at the photo there were three men standing in the shadows of the dead bodies. All three of them were posing with pistols in their hands. I could tell instantly that the three men in the picture were the same three men standing in front of me.

The men in front of me were all killers. They had killed this woman and her child. Seeing the picture of them standing over the bodies made me afraid. I wasn't afraid for myself. I was afraid for Diana and her son.

The man continued his questioning, "Earlier I asked you a question and you refused to answer. I'm going to ask you again. What do you think plan B is?"

I angrily responded, "What do you want from me? You break into my room and ask me all these questions and then you show me pictures of a dead woman and her child. What do y'all want from me and who are you guys?"

The men then looked at each other and one of them said, "We are the three little pigs, and you are the big bad wolf." Then they all laughed.

He said, "In the story, the three pigs-built houses that they thought would keep them safe from the wolf. But in the

153

end the wolf ate them all. You know why he ate all of them?"

"No," I said. "Why?"

He chuckled, "Because they are pigs and wolves love pork." Then the three men laughed again.

He said, "You're going to be our big bad wolf. But instead of eating the little pigs, you are going to keep them safe. You will keep us from eating them. The woman and the boy are your little pigs.

"If plan B doesn't work, we will kill them both. They will be dead tonight. And you will be left alive. We will spare you and leave you to go to their funerals knowing that you could have been their hero wolf.

"But instead, you were their bad wolf. The big bad wolf who let them get eaten. Do you understand my analogy?"

I shook my head yes in agreement. I knew these guys meant business. I had to come up with something fast. They weren't going to take no for an answer. I had to tell them who I was and why I was there. If I didn't, they said they would kill Diana and her son, and I believed them." The clock was ticking, and I didn't have time to waste.

The man urged me to talk. He said, "This is your last chance to tell us what we want to know. Or we will leave you here and pay a visit to the woman and her son."

I knew this was it. I blurted out the best thing I could think of and hoped it would make sense.

I said, "Well, the truth is I'm here because something happened to me. My mother left me when I was a small child, and I was raised by my grandmother. She is an elderly woman and is one of the wealthiest people in our town.

"She is rich and has acres of land and several businesses worth millions. She has a lot of money. But she is very ill. The doctors have given her less than a month to live.

154

"And a few days ago, she called me into her room and showed me her will. She told me that she was leaving behind a legacy of wealth and made me pledge to her that I would not squander it. She told me the land belonged to our family and that I must never sell it, and I agreed not to.

"But when she showed me her will, it had two names on it. My name and the name of a man who I had never met. She told me to find this man. She told me the name on the will was the name of my long-lost brother.

"She said it was not his fault that we didn't know each other. She said he has no idea who I am, but my task was to find him and let him know about his inheritance. So, I researched the man's name and I found him.

"He is the man who sits on the jury. That man is my half-brother and she left half of her inheritance to him. "So that's why I'm here. That's why I'm in disguise.

"That's why every day at trial I only focused on him. I can't believe my grandmother would leave half her fortune to a man she never knew. It disgusts me every time I see him.

"I can't stand the thought of giving millions of dollars to a stranger. Blood or not, he's no kin to me or my grandmother. He's an imposter. I'm undercover while I try to prove that he is a fraud. That's why I'm here."

Then one of the men replied, "Wow… that is an amazing story. To see a man so dedicated that he comes to this small town to investigate a stranger. A man who your grandmother says is your brother. If I had a brother I never met and I found out he was going to inherit my money I would be pissed too.

"You do know that he is not going to turn down that money, right? When he finds out he has millions, he's going to do everything he can to get it. I don't care what you say or how you say it, he is going to want your money. No one turns down money."

155

Then the other man chimed in, "So what are you going to do if he is not a fraud? If he is indeed your brother, are you going to split your inheritance with a stranger? I can understand your grandmother wanting to help him but giving half her fortune to him is foolish. That's your money. It belongs to you. All of it."

I agreed with them both and nodded my head to almost everything they said. They not only believed the story I just told them, but they sympathized with me. They saw no right in my grandmother's request. Only wrong.

At this point I wasn't afraid anymore. I knew I couldn't trust them, but now I felt like I could at least talk to them. I now saw this as an opening to ask them questions. I wanted to know who they were and why they targeted me.

I asked, "So now that we are clear. Now that you know why I am here. Can you do the same? Can you tell me why you are here? Why you pointed a gun at me and why you showed me the pictures of those people.

"And please spare me the three pigs and bad wolf analogy. Just be honest with me and tell me who you guys are."

At this point the man standing closest to me sat on the edge of the bed while the other men continued to stand. He was trying to present himself as someone I could trust.

He said, "We are... how should I say? We are investors. We have invested a lot of time and money into a product that is worth millions of dollars, and we will do everything we can to make sure we see a return on our investment.

"Mr. Cordova, the man sitting on trial, he is our boss. We have worked with him and been by his side since we were teenage boys in Colombia. You see, Mr. Cordova has a lot of people in my country who depend on him. People who need him to come back home to finish what he started.

"He has transformed the lives of many people and we have to make sure he returns home to Colombia. We have to make sure we keep our investment safe.
If he is found guilty all hell will break loose.

"Not only has he threatened to unleash a tidal wave of evidence that will implicate members of your government, but he is an innocent man who your country is trying to crucify. If he is found guilty, he will surely die in your American prison. And we will not let that happen.

"So, we did our research. We looked at every member of the jury. We have all of their names and addresses. We have everything we need. Your American government gave us this information. They do not want this case to go to the jury.

"They want this over. So they are secretly helping us. They want to make sure Mr. Cordova is not found guilty. So the tapes don't get released. If we can get him off, the tapes will be destroyed. And that is what everyone wants.

"Our job is to find a juror who can be swayed to stand alone amid a mountain of evidence. Evidence that they say proves Julius is guilty. So we have to find a juror who will vote not guilty in spite of the pressure and evidence all around him.

"We need to find someone who has something to lose. Someone who can be swayed. We followed you because we know you have an interest in juror number three. Your frustrations were becoming more noticeable.

"We know that something about him has bothered you and we are glad we found you. We believe you can help us. With a little persuasion we think you can get juror number three to be our sympathizer.

"At some point every man will bend. Every man will break. Especially a man with a beautiful woman and child like juror number three has. I think we can work together to get us both what we want."

I replied, "Oh yeah, well what do you want me to do? I'm done with this trial. I was heading outta this town today before you guys busted in here. I can't speak to him. I can't get close to him. I don't know what I was thinking coming here. With all the security there's no way to get near him or any of the jurors."

One of the men said, "So we understand that. We understand your frustrations. We have been looking at the situation just as you have. We have been going to court every day just like you. Standing in line every morning, just like you.

"We have been doing the same thing. While you were studying juror number three, we studied all of them. Trying to see which one we could target. Waiting for an opportunity to strike. And now we have one. And you... you have been waiting for an opportunity as well. And now you have one.

"We all have one. We have an opportunity to work together to get what we want. Either you can walk away and let your inheritance be split with a stranger or you can take action. We know you have not been coming here and spending all your time here for nothing. You are clearly a man on a mission. We will help you.

"It seems you need a plan to eliminate your frustrations. You need a plan to get and keep what's rightfully yours. We will see to it that this problem of yours goes away. We handle problems like yours all the time."

I nodded my head in agreement and asked, "But how do you plan to do that? No one is allowed to get close to the jurors. You can't even speak to them. They are sequestered at a hotel with heavy security. They have police and FBI agents around them all day. Security is everywhere."

158

He replied, "Well, you let us worry about that. Remember, we have people all around the courthouse who will help us. Your government does not want a guilty verdict. We have sympathizers. We have people to help make things happen.

"So, to be clear, we will put together a plan that works for both of us. But you need to understand that what we are doing for you is a courtesy. This request we have is non-negotiable. We will get from you what we came here for.

"And we didn't come here to ask for your help. We came here to tell you what you must do. The pictures I showed you, those pictures are of the people juror number three values.

"He will do as he is instructed once he is aware of what's at stake. And just like you, he doesn't have a choice. If he refuses, we will kill his woman and her child and we will let him live to see it.

"He will live to attend their funerals. And then we will kill him. And we like you. But if you don't do as you are told we will also kill you too.

"And don't take it personal. It's just business. We are businessmen and we have a job to do. And It's very important that you do as you are told. Just follow our directives and you will be fine.

"You work for us now. Everything you do, every place you go will be ordered by us. And that means no more going to court. There will be no more trips to the courthouse for you.

"No more trips anywhere. You will not leave this room until you are instructed to do so. Where are your car keys? Hand them over to me."

I complied and hesitantly handed over my keys to the man.

He said, "One of my men will be stationed outside this hotel room. You may not leave this room for any reason whatsoever. We will bring you food or whatever you need. This trial is supposed to last another week and we have little time to waste.

"We will come back to see you tomorrow with your first instructions. Until then do not destroy your disguise. Keep safe your fake mustache, wig, and glasses. You will need them again. You will need them very soon.

"But we must be clear. If you attempt to leave this room, we will kill you. And our plan will still get done. With you dead or alive our work will still get done."

After hearing all his orders, I interrupted him and said, "Well what if I told you I'm not going to stay locked in this room like a prisoner. What if I told you I'm not sitting in this room for a whole week. And that I don't need permission to leave. I'll do what you say I need to do, but I'm not gonna stay locked in this room for who knows how long."

The man replied, "Well if you feel that way that's your right. But I don't believe you are a tough guy. I don't believe you came all this way to lose your life over a man you despise. I don't believe you want to end up like the woman and child in the picture we showed you earlier.

"But I could be wrong. If you desire to be a tough guy, if that's your plan all you have to do is step foot outside of this room. If you are a tough guy like you say, you can prove it. When we leave… you can leave. We'll see how far you get with a bullet in your head.

"I'm taking your car keys, your cell phone and this hotel phone. We are leaving now. We will hope to see you tomorrow. But if we don't, it was a pleasure speaking to you. And remember what we said, with or without your assistance we will get the job done."

As the men left the hotel room, I realized I was in way too deep. I had found myself fully engrossed in some type of mob circle. I never envisioned something like this happening.

As much as I despised J3 I didn't want to see any harm to Diana or her son. I didn't want to hurt them. I realized I had to do what the men instructed me to do.

I had no choice but to follow their orders. And the men were right. I didn't come all this way to put my life in danger and I certainly didn't come all this way to bring harm to Diana. I loved her and I would do whatever I could to keep her safe.

While pacing back and forth in the hotel room I began to think of myself as a hero. I thought of myself as the hero wolf the man described. Someone who was going to save the day. I was turning a bad situation into something good.

I also began to think of the men as a blessing. If they could get J3 out of the way, then I could have Diana. I could live the life I dreamed of with the woman of my dreams. Maybe this was truly a blessing. Maybe the men were not bad guys but a blessing in disguise. Maybe, just maybe all of this could turn out in my favor.

The men needed me, and I needed them. And Diana needed me to do the right thing. She needed me more than she would ever know. I spent the next couple hours pacing back and forth in that hotel room.

With each hour, the room seemed smaller and smaller, and I felt more and more confined. I turned on the TV then I turned it off. Then an hour later I turned it back on then quickly turned it back off. I was bored. Bored out of my mind.

Being stuck in this room was punishment and I wanted out. But I knew if I stepped foot out the door I would surely be shot. I knew somewhere out there was an assassin waiting to test his marksmanship. But he wouldn't get the opportunity to test it on me.

After another hour I turned the TV on again. This time I turned to the news and sure enough a news flash popped up. It was about Mr. Cordova's trial. It was breaking news.

The broadcast said that the prosecution attorneys have notified the judge that they have rested their case. They were done early. The trial was moving along much quicker than anyone expected.

After only four days, the trial was handed to the defense. The reporter said this announcement shocked everyone in the courtroom. With this update the case could be handed to the jury in as little as three days. He said the trial would be coming to an end early next week, leaving many to wonder what was really going on inside the courtroom. The reporter said Mr. Cordova's attorneys were extremely confident that their client would be found not guilty.

Hearing that the case was moving faster than expected created even more anxiety for me. Why was Mr. Cordova's case moving so quickly? The prosecution must know something no one else knows.

Perhaps his attorneys know that the men who visited my room have a plan and feel confident that it will work. Perhaps they notified the prosecution that they have a plan for an acquittal. The attorneys must know something that no one else knows.

I sat on the edge of the bed and wondered what in the world I had gotten myself into. I wondered what instructions the men would bring tomorrow. I wondered what they had planned for me. Whatever it was, I was ready to hear it.

I realized the whole time I had been here I hadn't planned anything, so I was curious what type of plan they could come up with. Surely it would be better than mine. As the evening wore along the clock seemed to move at a turtle's pace. Each minute seemed like an hour and each hour seemed like a day.

I was bored and I was restless. I hated being in this small room. I had nothing to do but think. Sometimes that can be good and sometimes that can be bad. But whatever the case, I couldn't help but think about their plan for me.

I also wondered if the men really had someone outside my room ready to shoot me if I attempted to leave. I wouldn't dare open the door to find out. I was terrified of the thought of being shot. And the thought of being shot as soon as I opened the door was even more frightening.

But I was curious to know if someone was really out there. Fearing what might happen if I opened the door, I decided to peek through the curtains instead. I just wanted to see the parking lot. I wanted to see if my car was still out there. I wanted to see what was going on out there.

I wanted to put my eyes on something other than the objects in this room. So
I slowly pulled back the curtains and I noticed the parking lot looked a lot like it did every night I had been here. My car was parked in the same spot I parked it earlier. But my car wasn't alone.

It literally wasn't alone. There appeared to be a man sitting in the front seat of my car. He was sitting in my car and staring straight ahead at my room. For a second I believe he noticed me peeking out from the curtains because he quickly opened the driver's side door and stepped out.

When I saw him step out, I immediately closed the curtains and resumed my pacing back and forth in my room. I don't know what the man did after that, but I wouldn't dare peek out the curtains again to find out.

That night I didn't sleep very well but I did drift off at some point in the middle of the night. And then I awoke at five thirty in the morning. This was the same time I had awakened for the past five days. At this point my body was trained to get up early.

My body and mind were preparing for court. But this time when I woke up, I wasn't ironing my clothes or getting ready for court. I wasn't doing anything because I had nowhere to go. So, I turned up the volume on the TV and turned again to the news. Within minutes I got another update on the trial of Mr. Cordova. The news basically said the same thing they reported last night.

That the prosecution had rested early, and this trial would be wrapping up much sooner than anyone expected. He also reiterated the fact that no one could understand why the prosecution had rested so early in such a powerful case. No one could figure out what to make of this sudden change in the strategy.

As I sat on the end of the bed watching the news a sudden unexpected knock on the door startled me and completely caught me off guard. It alarmed me. With everything that was going on I was afraid. Who would be knocking on my door at 5:30 in the morning?

My heart was beating fast, and I was afraid to go anywhere near the door. I didn't know if I should answer it or not. Why would anyone be knocking on my door this early in the morning? I sat on the edge of the bed and didn't budge.

I was too afraid to move. And after the first three knocks there was an eerie silence. I didn't make a move or make the slightest sound. And there was no noise or sounds coming from the other side of the door.

Was this the hit man I saw sitting in my car last night? What could he want with me? I did as they instructed me. I

164

didn't step foot out the door. I made no attempts to leave my room. Why would he be knocking?

My mind raced with a million thoughts. Then after at least ten seconds of silence there were three more knocks. And then another ten seconds to fifteen seconds of silence. And then three more knocks. And then... more silence.

But after the third set of knocks the door knocking stopped. Next, there was a light tapping on the window. It was a long steady tap. And each tap on the window was light and with just enough force that it would only disturb the person in the room. I still didn't move or budge.

And then the taps grew longer. I knew I had to do something. This had been going on for several minutes now. Whoever was on the other side of the door knew I was in here and they weren't leaving. So, I got up and tiptoed to the door to ask who it was. My voice was faint and fragile as I said, "Who is it?"

Then after a short pause the voice on the other end said, "It's the three little pigs, open the door."

I knew what that meant and who it was. The three little pigs were a reference made by the three men who paid me a visit yesterday. The men who worked for Mr. Cordova. They told me they would come back when they had instructions for me, but I didn't think they would be coming back at 5:30 in the morning.

I slid open the side curtain and saw that indeed it was the three men who had returned. As nervous as I was, I knew I had to open the door. Part of me felt this was not going to end well because nothing about this situation felt right.

I thought for sure they had come to kill me. But I couldn't do anything at this point but open the door and greet my potential killers. When I opened the door, the men were dressed just as they were yesterday. They had on dress

165

pants and polo shirts and were neat and well groomed, which was a good thing for me. Had they showed up in jeans and t-shirts I would have been much more worried.

As they walked into the room, they didn't brandish a pistol like they did the day before. And when all three were inside, I closed the door and took a seat in the same chair I sat in yesterday. The three men stood while I sat.

It was an awkward feeling as I was sitting down staring at them while they were all standing close together staring at me. Neither party said a word for several seconds. It was a weird experience. I wanted to say something, but I didn't know what to say. Then one of the men broke the tension by asking me a question.

He said, "Did you sleep well last night?"

I replied, "I slept about as good as the man sitting in my car watching me. How did he sleep last night?"

Then the man said, "Well we told him you were a tough guy. That you were gonna come out of the room and challenge him. So he waited on you. He waited all night. But he said you never came out.

"He was hoping you would open the door but we're glad you didn't. It's better to see you this way than laying on the ground dead. I think you made a good decision."

I interrupted him and said "All right already. I got it. Enough of the macho talk. I know why you guys are here. What's the plan? I wanna hear the plan. What are we gonna do? What do I have to do? I can't sit in this room all day doing nothing. I'm ready."

The man said, Well, that's very good. I'm glad to hear you say that because we are ready as well. I am going to tell you a very detailed plan. It's a plan for you to get into your brother's hotel room. His hotel room at the Clarion Hotel."

Chapter 21

Time For Action

He said, "You must listen carefully. Everything must go exactly as we tell you. We will only get one crack. There can be no hiccups. No cold feet. And if you do this correctly, in a couple days the jury will come to a decision everyone will be happy with."

I interrupted again and said, "Okay. So, if this plan works, Mr. Cordova will be free. But what about me? What am I getting out of this? What's in it for me?"

The man replied, "My friend, one thing we told you is we are businessmen. This is a business transaction. In order for a businessman to have a good name he must do good business. He must have a good product. My word is my product.

"When I give it to you, it's the most important thing I have. My word must be sufficient. We will take care of you and your problem. You must trust us. But now we must go over the plan. We must go over the details.

"So listen carefully. We don't write things down. Everything goes into the head. You must process what we tell you to perfection. One tiny error and everything is ruined, and the plan is dead.

"So you must listen. Clear your head and listen. Are we clear?"

I said, "Yes, we're good. I'm ready, go ahead."

He shook his head in agreement and said "Good, this is the plan and steps you will take:

1. At 6:30 in the morning you will arrive at the Clarion Hotel down the street from the courthouse. You will be in disguise. The same disguise you have been wearing in the courtroom.

2. When you arrive, you will park in the rear of the hotel and then go in through the main lobby. You will flash your hotel room key and the attendant will let you pass.

3. You will then walk straight ahead toward the elevator. You will push the elevator button and then stand next to it. When the door opens do not go inside. Walk away and go to the restroom down the hall. When inside the restroom, find a stall and stay there until 7:00 a.m.

4. At 7:00 you will take off your disguise and leave the bathroom. You will turn right and walk straight. You will walk past the elevator and keep walking to the other side of the hallway. All the jurors are staying on the first floor in rooms along this part of the hallway.

5. There will be a sheriff's deputy in the middle of the hallway. He will be sitting at a table and will stop you before you enter that part of the hallway. He will probably be reading his newspaper and sipping a cup of coffee like he does every morning.

6. This is the juror check in table. No one but jurors are allowed to enter this portion of the hallway. When you approach the table, the deputy will pull out a tablet and scan your face.

7. After he scans you, you can move freely down the hallway. Your brother's room is room 108. Here is your room key. It's the same key you will flash to the receptionist when you enter the hotel.

8. At 6:45 all the jurors leave their rooms and meet to have breakfast together in a banquet room at the hotel. Every morning they eat together for thirty minutes. The room will be empty for fifteen minutes.
9. At 7:00 when you enter the hotel room you will hide in the closet next to the door. You will stay there until your brother comes in at 7:15. You will have exactly fifteen minutes from the time he enters the room to tell him what he needs to know.
10. At 7:30 the jurors meet at the end of the hallway and are escorted to a shuttle bus that takes them to the courthouse. At 7:45 they leave.
11. At 8:15 you will leave the room and exit out the door at the end of the hallway. The deputy in the hallway and check in station will be gone by then. They are always gone by 8:00 but to be safe you must stay in the room until 8:15.
12. Everything this jury does is scripted to the minute. The police and FBI are with them at all times. When they leave the hotel the police and agents all leave too. So when you leave his room at 8:15 everyone will be gone, and you will be fine.

Do you understand everything? It's very important that you do this right."

I shook my head and said "Yes, I understand."

He said, "Good. So here is the next part. When your brother enters the room, you must pull out a pistol and tell him to not make a sound. If you do not pull a pistol, he will surely try to fight you and that will not be good. You must immediately take control of the situation.

"Let him know that his life is in danger. Tell him this is a life-or-death situation. Tell him it involves not only him but the woman he loves and her son. Tell him he must listen carefully to you.

"Let him know that you do not have a lot of time to talk. Try your best to calm him down. He will surely be caught off guard and will be nervous and afraid.

"Once he calms down, tell him to take a seat. When he sits down you can lower your pistol. People are much easier to control when they are seated. Now tell him your story.

"Tell him your grandmother is dying and is on her deathbed. And on her deathbed, she told you that you have a brother. A brother you have never met or knew anything about. Tell him she asked you to find him, and you gave her your word you would.

"Then tell him that while you were visiting your grandmother three men approached you at the hospital and threatened you. Tell him the three men know about him and that he is a member of the jury. Tell him we know about all of his family members and that's how we found you at the hospital.

"Let him know that we threatened you. Tell him we will kill you, him, and everyone he cares about if he does not follow our orders. Then take out this folder with these pictures of his woman and her son. Give them to him. Let him see them.

"Let him know that if he does not do exactly as he is told the men will kill them both. Tell him that he must make sure that Mr. Cordova is not found guilty. He must not vote to convict. When the jury is handed the case, he must vote not guilty.

"Tell him no matter how much evidence he sees he must find flaws. He must not vote guilty. Tell him he does not need to persuade the other jurors.

"Explain to him that it only takes one juror to not agree and then we have a hung jury. He needs to be that one juror. We need this to be a hung jury. Did you copy all that?" I shook my head again and said "Yes. I copy."

Then he continued, "Good. Now here is the last part. Let him know that after the verdict is announced he is not to talk to anyone. When the hung jury verdict is read, he must not speak to any reporters, and he is not to call anyone on his phone.

"Tell him thirty minutes after the verdict is released, he will meet you outside the hotel at the bus stop on the corner of Anderson and Dixon Avenue. Tell him he is to pick you up in his car and after he picks you up you will give him his next instructions.

"Tell him you will give him information about his family and let him know that after he does this no harm will come to them. Make sure he understands what is required of him. He must understand that if he does not do as he is told we will kill him. Do you understand these instructions? Can you remember all of that?"

I said "Yes, I understand everything. But what happens when he picks me up at the bus stop. What happens after that?"

Then the man said, "Well that is the part where I step in and keep my word. Your problem will no longer be a problem. When he picks you up at the bus stop, I will be with you. He will be picking us both up. Tell him the only thing he needs to do is follow the car in front of him.

"After he does that, your problem will be solved, and we won't be needing each other anymore. Let's just put it like that."

I nodded my head and said "I got it. So what day are we gonna do this? How much time do we have?"

The man interrupted me and said, "What do you mean how much time do we have? And what day? What day do you think? We don't have time to waste. This will happen today. It's almost 6:00 already. You need to get yourself together and head to the Clarion Hotel. You need to be there by 6:30 a.m.

"Remember what I told you. Follow the time schedule and everything will be fine. Here is your room key. After you do this, come back here. You must come back to this hotel room without delay.

"And then you must not leave here until the verdict is released. And after they announce it, you must make your way to the courthouse and meet me at the bus stop I discussed. Are we clear? This must happen today."

I told him, "I got it. I will be ready. But what if I need to get in touch with you? After I do this, what if I need things? There is no food in this room. No food or water. How can I find you?"

He said, "We will take care of that. You just make sure you do what we discussed. I will see you soon. Until then just know that Mr. Cordova will be forever grateful for your service."

And then the three men left. Just like that. They were gone and the clock was ticking. They had a plan that I was going to execute. The whole time I was here I couldn't plan anything. And now I was getting ready for one of the biggest challenges of my life.

I had to get this right. This was gonna be difficult, but I was ready for the challenge. The day had finally come. I would finally come face to face with J3 and his fate would be in my hands.

The Colombians made a deal with me that if I got J3 to throw the jury they would take care of my problem. J3 was definitely my problem. He stood in the way of what I wanted. He stood in my way of getting Diana.

The woman who I had dreamt about and then miraculously came into existence. I had convinced myself that J3 was undeserving of Diana. I had watched for days as he flirted with the young juror next to him in court seeming to care the least about Diana. I watched as he carried himself like a man with no morals. A man with no principles.

I had convinced myself that he and the young juror were romantically involved. I had convinced myself that J3 was undeserving of Diana and had to be taken out of the picture. But I never really thought about what that meant. What did remove him consist of?

Would the Colombians threaten him like they did me? What was their plan for him? They said he would no longer be my problem. Part of me knew what that meant but the other part of me wanted to think that maybe it meant something else. The more I thought about it, I didn't care. I just wanted him out of the picture.

As I put on my clothes and prepared to leave, I realized that I had orchestrated an act that would almost certainly result in J3 being harmed. And then I thought about the possibility that I might be harmed too. What if the Colombians decided to do away with both of us?

What if after J3 threw the jury they decided to do away with us both. If they wanted to avoid any heat coming their way their best option was to remove both of us. But I didn't think that would happen. They assumed that J3 was my long-lost brother who I wanted out of the picture so he wouldn't get a part of his inheritance.

That's what they thought because that's what I told them. And they believed it. So I felt pretty good that no harm would come my way.

And eliminating a juror was sure to raise suspicions. Perhaps they didn't plan on harming him. Maybe they were gonna make sure he wanted no part of my grandmother's money. Maybe their plan for J3 was to make sure he would never attempt to claim the money my grandmother supposedly was leaving him.

These were very wealthy businesspeople and Mr. Cordova was a drug lord. A kingpin. Maybe they planned to offer J3 a large sum of money in return for his not guilty verdict. The more I thought about it the more I felt that was probably the plan they had for him. They had money and would offer it to him.

In their mind my problem with him was a financial problem. With all the money they had I was confident that was their plan. To offer him a lump sum of money in return for his service. J3 was gonna be fine.

But I still needed him out of the picture. And them giving him money would not solve my problems with him and Diana. So I had to hope and wait and see how this turned out. I really wanted him gone and I needed the Colombians to find a way to make that happen.

J3 was sure to be at the center of controversy. The sheer magnitude of being the only juror who refused to find guilt in one of the most corrupt mobsters and international crime boss trials could not be overstated. J3's life was sure to change.

His phone was almost certain to be bugged, his home would be under surveillance and his every move would be watched. His life would be lived under the microscope of suspicion.

While there is no crime for voting not guilty, there is absolutely a crime to be a financially motivated juror. So if the Colombians gave him any money the FBI would definitely find out. And that would not be good for J3.

174

He couldn't spend it. And if he did he would have to explain where he got it. So the more I thought about it the more I realized the Colombians had no plans to offer J3 any money.

It would raise too many red flags. J3's fate was sealed. He was definitely going to be eliminated. I knew it for sure now... but I still didn't care. I just wanted this whole ordeal to be over with and for him to be out of my way.

It was 6:00 a.m. when I left my hotel room and headed toward the Clarion Motel. When I arrived at the hotel it was 6:20. I drove to the back of the hotel and parked in the rear as I had been instructed to. I had already put on my disguise at my hotel, so I looked at my face in the rear-view mirror and made sure everything was in place like it needed to be. I sat in the car for almost ten minutes then at 6:29 a.m. I walked around to the main entrance.

When I walked through the lobby I walked right past the reception desk, waved at the attendant, and flashed my room key, then kept walking. I quickly made my way to the elevator which was directly ahead of me.

Once at the elevator I hit the button and waited for the elevator to appear. As I waited for the elevator I glanced to the right and could see a police officer seated at a makeshift check in counter down the hallway. I knew that would be the hallway I would go down thirty minutes from now.

I didn't have long to wait for the elevator. Within seconds of me pressing the button the elevator doors opened. But instead of going inside I quickly walked to the men's restroom which was a few feet away on the left. Once inside the restroom I found a stall and stayed there until it was time for me to leave.

It was quiet there and the time went by faster than I expected. I was nervous but I wasn't afraid. I just wanted to get this over with. I just wanted to deliver the message to J3 and get back to my hotel room.

At 7:00 a.m. I took off my mustache, fake wig and clear glasses and threw them in the bathroom garbage can. Then I left the bathroom and made my way down the long hallway. When I walked to the other side an officer greeted me at the check in table.

Other than saying good morning he didn't say anything else. He took out a small tablet, held it to my face and then after a beep, he told me I was good. I quickly walked down the hallway and entered room 108.

When inside the room I did exactly as I was told. I hid in the closet next to the door and waited until J3 arrived. My heart was beating fast. After what seemed like an eternity, when I looked at my watch it was 7:15 a.m.

J3 had not arrived yet but I knew at any moment he would walk through that door. I knew this would be my first chance to see him and I had to get it right. I had to be ready. Any second now J3 would enter the room.

Then I reached behind my back and grabbed the pistol the Colombians gave me. I held it firmly in my right hand and waited for J3 to enter. Then at 7:18 a.m. I heard the door open. I waited two or three seconds after it closed then I immediately emerged from behind the door and pointed the gun at his face.

I told him to have a seat on the bed and to not say a word. He was completely caught off guard and quickly sat down as he had been ordered. He looked as if he had seen a ghost. He was terrified. When he looked at me, he didn't say a word, but I could tell he was shocked that we looked so much alike.

And I knew the fear he was experiencing because I felt the same thing when the Colombians entered my room and pointed their gun at me. I knew exactly how he felt so as soon as he sat down, I lowered my pistol. I lowered my pistol and told him who I was and why I was there.

Then I took the pictures out of the folder and gave them to him. I told him everything I was told to tell him. Initially he didn't say a word. He just looked at me. As if he was in complete disbelief.

He said he understood the story I explained to him about my grandmother, but he said his only concern was for Diana and her son. The only thing he asked me was if she was okay and if she knew what was going on.

Then he asked me if I could give him my word that nothing bad would happen to her when this was over. I told him she was fine and that nothing would happen if he did as he was instructed. I told him he had to hang the jury by voting not guilty.

He nodded his head in agreement and said he would. He said for me to tell the Colombians he would do it. I told him that was a good decision then I told him where to meet me after the verdict was read.

I told him after the verdict that he couldn't talk to any reporters or talk to anyone on his phone, and he nodded in agreement again and said he understood. Then I told him I couldn't leave his room until after he and the other jurors left for the trial. I told him I had to stay in his room until 8:15 a.m. He shook his head again and said okay. And that was it.

For the five or so remaining minutes we were together in his room we didn't say a word to each other. It was a quiet, nerve-wracking experience and when he finally left the room, I felt relieved. I had done what I set out to do. I had done my part. Now everything was in motion. I couldn't wait to get back to my room.

I was mentally and physically exhausted. When 8:15 hit I left his room and went out the side exit door at the end of the hallway. When I got in my car I sat back and took a

177

deep breath. I was relieved that that was over. When I got back to my room, to my surprise there were several packs of lunch meat, fruits, chips, and bottles of water on my bed. The Colombians had loaded me up with food and things I needed so I wouldn't have to leave the room. It was officially the waiting period. All I could do was wait.

So every day over the next couple of days I was glued to the news. I anxiously waited for the case to come to a conclusion. Then after three long days of waiting all sides had rested and the case was given to the jury. The jury was in deliberation. All I needed was for J3 to come through like he was told. All he had to do was say not guilty.

I knew that would not be an easy task. The government had presented an airtight case, and everyone knew Mr. Cordova was guilty. And during the trial his legal team was quiet. They made no threats to release their supposedly damaging videos if he was found guilty.

His lawyers, publicist and representatives were surprisingly confident that he would be acquitted. It was like they knew something no one else knew. They knew there was no need for them to make threats to release the damaging videos because they didn't need to.

They knew he was gonna be free because they had someone on the inside. They knew they had a corrupt juror. All they had to do was sit back and wait for the verdict. They were confident things would go their way.

And the prosecution must have known something too. They rested their case after only four days. They must have been tipped off that the trial would not go as they had hoped and maybe they decided to save some of their evidence for a new trial that would come if this one resulted in a hung jury.

And then after three long days of jury deliberations it was announced that a verdict was in and would be read today. The verdict was finally in and would be read tonight at 8:00 p.m.

It was 6:00 in the evening and soon I would be getting ready to head to the bus stop to meet J3. I was ready to go now but I didn't want to sit and wait at the bus stop for two hours. So I waited a little longer in my room. Then at 7:30 p.m. I left and made my way to the bus stop across the street from the courthouse.

When I arrived at the bus stop one of the Colombians was already there. He didn't say a word to me, he just stood there staring at the traffic. He and I were the only two people there and we didn't have to wait long to get what we were there for.

At 8:00 p.m. the verdict was read. The jury foreman read the verdict to the court. He said the jury could not reach a unanimous agreement and therefore could not agree on a verdict. The judge was not happy with the jury but all he could do was to declare the trial a mistrial.

Then the judge asked the prosecutors if they planned to retry the defendant and they stated that they did. The judge then announced that a new trial date would be set soon but in the meantime the defendant was to be released immediately on bail. And just like that, it was over. Mr. Cordova was a free man.

Shortly after the verdict was announced the jury foreman went on TV and told the world what went wrong in deliberations. He went on national television and announced that all but one juror voted to convict. And because they could not get a unanimous agreement a mistrial was the result.

He didn't say the jurors name but his press conference all but sealed J3's fate. The whole of the U.S. criminal and judicial systems were officially thrown in a loop. The world was watching, and America had gotten it wrong.

Our judicial system had failed, and an international crime boss was back on the streets and there was nothing anyone could do about it. When people find out it was J3 who sabotaged the trial he is sure to go down as the most unethical juror in the history of American law.

Over the years there have been hundreds of verdicts that stunned the public, but none stung more so than this one. It seemed as if the jury foreman knew the magnitude of this verdict and was trying to get in front of it. He wanted the world to know it wasn't him or the other jurors who got this wrong.

He wanted everyone to know that it was the result of one person. One person alone did this. And it wouldn't be long before the government came looking for that one person. After the verdict, all the jurors were in front of cameras talking to reporters. All of them were doing interviews. All of them except juror number three.

He was on his way to meet me at the bus stop. He was on his way to get his next set of instructions. He was trying to find out what else he needed to do to keep his family safe.

Chapter 22

Keeping His Word

As I sat at the bus stop waiting for J3 I felt relieved to hear the verdict. I knew that whatever happened to J3 he had brought it upon himself. He was single-handedly the voice of opposition amid a room of certainty. He made his own bed and now he had to lay in it.

I convinced myself a long time ago that J3 was a man of poor judgment and now his lack of judgment would be his downfall. What I failed to acknowledge was that I had been the reason for his poor judgment. My mind didn't register the fact that I had corrupted his thought process when I entered his hotel room and delivered a threatening message to him.

I had seemingly convinced myself that J3's fate was his own even though I had stalked him for almost a week in the courtroom. I convinced myself that I didn't care about him and that I only cared about Diana. And every time I thought about her, I reminded myself that he was the only thing that stood in my way.

As I sat on the bench and my mind wandered, I almost forgot that I was not alone. Standing a few feet away from me was one of the Colombians. And while I daydreamed about Diana, he stared at the traffic and kept looking at his watch, constantly checking it and then spitting his chewing tobacco on the ground.

Every few minutes he would check his watch then spit on the ground again. He was steady and focused. I thought by now he would have talked to me or made a comment about Mr. Cordova's trial. But he showed no sign of excitement or even a willingness to talk.

For the majority of the time we were together at the bus stop he never said a word. But then after ten or fifteen minutes of silence he spoke to me, and surprisingly he had a few supportive words to say.

He said, "Remember... have him follow the car in front of him. Make sure he does that."
I looked at him and I nodded my head in agreement.

Then he said, "And also... you did good. You did good kid. You kept your word. Now I'm gonna keep mine. When he picks us up, don't do a lot of talking. Don't say much. If he asks you questions, don't answer. Just tell him to follow the car. Tell him we will explain everything. That's all you have to do."

And that was it. The whole time we were at the bus stop that was all he said to me. And that was all the conversation I needed. When he told me I did good it made me feel good. I felt like I was a part of the team.

Like I was a part of his organization. Though I knew little of the man who stood a few feet away from me I felt at ease in his presence. His calm demeanor and his constant focus made me feel safe. I felt like I was in good hands.

As we waited for J3 I looked around for the car that he was supposed to follow but I didn't see anything. I assumed the vehicle would show up just as J3 arrived. But what if the vehicle was late. How was I supposed to tell J3 to follow a vehicle if it wasn't even there?

I wasn't gonna ask the Colombian what to do. He told me not to ask any questions. So if the car was late, I was just

182

gonna tell J3 to drive straight. You can't go wrong with going straight.

And then, just as it seemed like we had been waiting at the bus stop for an eternity, a car pulled up alongside us. When the passenger side window rolled down, I saw it was J3. All he said was, "Hey man, get in."

As I walked to the front passenger door the Colombian walked to the side rear passenger door. We both got in J3's car at the same time. As soon as we sat down J3 asked, "Who the hell is this guy?" But before anyone could answer, another car pulled up alongside us. I told J3 the man in the back seat was with me. Then I told him to follow the car in front of us.

As we followed the car, I remembered what the Colombian told me. Don't talk too much and don't answer any of J3's questions. When the car pulled up alongside us, the first thing J3 asked me was where we were going. And then he asked me again who the guy in the backseat was, and both times I didn't say a word. I just told him to follow the car in front of us.

I sat silently as I had been instructed. My silence, along with the silence of the Colombian, had created a tense and nerve-wracking atmosphere. Not only for J3, but for myself too. The more J3 repeatedly asked the same questions about where we were going the longer the silence fell.

I couldn't answer him because I didn't know. And I could tell he was becoming upset. His voice had gone from worry and confusion to anger. He said to me, "Look man, you need to tell me something! You need to tell me right now where we are going and who this guy is in the backseat. If you don't tell me, I'm pulling this car over!"

Then the dreaded silence returned. But this time it only lasted for a few seconds. Just as J3 looked to his right as if he was going to pull over on the side of the road the Colombian began to speak.

He said, "You repeatedly ask who I am, but it doesn't matter. No one in this car knows my name. No one in this car will ever know my name. It's not important. What is important is that you follow the car in front of you. What you have done today is quite remarkable. You did something that has never been done before.

"You stood up for what was right, and a powerful man will be freed. There will be people from your country who will try to ruin your life. They will surround your home with cameras, they will tap your phone lines, they will follow you around with undercover agents and try to destroy you.

"You see, in your country your government has too much power. When they want you, they get you and they cannot handle rejection. And you rejected them today. You rejected American democracy.

"And your government will not take this blow lightly. In my country the government is weak. People can be bought. They are often harmed and threatened if they don't comply. People with money and power are never guilty.

"But in America things are different. Money does not always win your freedom. If your government believes you are guilty there is no hope for justice. And your government believed Mr. Cordova was guilty.

"They thought they had a good case. They had lots of evidence. Very good evidence. They thought they had him. They thought he was guilty. And then we found your brother. And when we found him, we found you.

"And we are glad we found the both of you because an innocent man is now free. Mr. Cordova will forever be grateful to the both of you."

Then J3 responded by saying, "Well I didn't sign up to be a part of this. I just wanna go home. I just wanna get away

184

from all of this. And I don't know this guy sitting next to me. This guy looks like me and claims to be my brother, but I don't know him. I don't trust him. And I don't know or trust you. So, when this is over, I just want my life back.

"I wanna go back home to the people I love. When this is over, I don't want anything to do with you, Mr. Cordova or this guy sitting next to me. Do you understand me? Do both of you understand me?

"I can't believe I'm in this mess. And that man was guilty. He hurt a lot of people. He's a drug dealer. He's a murderer. He exploits young girls and he's an international sex trafficker.

"That man should be in prison. I'm not proud of what I did today. I only did it to keep my family safe. That's it. That's the only reason I did this."

The whole time J3 was talking he continued to follow the car in front of him. It was nearing 8:30 p.m. and the sun had officially gone down. We had already been following the car for about fifteen minutes and J3 and the Colombian continued to have a dialogue with one another. I just sat silently and listened.

The Colombian said, "You shouldn't complain about things you can't control. At this point you are a hero to millions. Millions of people in my country will be forever grateful for your service. Mr. Cordova has asked me to deliver his gratitude. The car you are following has two men in it. They are my brothers. We have worked together for many years.

"In that car is a package for you. It's a gift from Mr. Cordova. You see, these people in your country will stop at nothing until they place you on the same stands as Mr. Cordova. They will not stop until they try and convict you the way they tried to convict him. They will stop at nothing to destroy you.

185

"Everyone will turn on you. You friends, your family, everyone. Mr. Cordova is offering you a home in our country. You will be treated like a king. All the money and earthly things you desire. It's all yours if you want it.

"That message is not from me, it's directly from him. He is offering to solve your problems in return for what you've done for him. You can come live in my country and have no worries for the rest of your life."

Then J3 said, "I don't want any money. I don't want Mr. Cordova's money. That money is dirty. That money isn't gonna do me any good right now. And I'm not leaving my country to go live somewhere else.

"My home is here. And how much further are we going? We've been driving for a long time. Where is this car taking us?"

The Colombian sat quietly as J3 continued to ramble and complain about his frustrations. We had been following this car for about twenty minutes and now it was very dark outside. We made several turns and neither J3 nor myself knew where we were or where we were going.

Then all of a sudden, we slowed down and pulled into what appeared to be a large industrial park. There were large trucks and warehouses everywhere and the streets were all very well lit. Nothing about this area felt odd or unsafe.

Then J3's nerves seemed to have calmed as he followed the car in front of us. He stopped complaining and just drove. We turned into a parking lot behind a large shipping warehouse, and he continued to follow the car in front of him until we reached the rear of the parking lot. It was 8:35 p.m. when both cars came to a halt.

The parking spaces next to the large buildings were all filled with cars but the area where we were parked was empty. We were parked in the back and at a great distance from the nearest building. It was dark outside, and we could

186

see several large warehouses, but they were nowhere close to where we were.

As we sat in the car we watched as the two men in the car in front of us exited their vehicle. When they got out of the car both men were holding large briefcases, and if I hadn't known any better, I would have thought this was some sort of illegal transaction. It looked like the makings of a drug deal.

I didn't know what was in the suitcases. I thought one might be a suitcase full of money for J3 and the other full of money for me. It appeared as if the Colombians wanted to reward us with money for helping them. I couldn't imagine anything else in those suitcases.

As the men approached the vehicle, they both laid their suitcases on the hood of J3's car and motioned for him to get out. J3 sat patiently in the car for a few seconds until the voice of the Colombian sitting in the backseat emerged. He spoke softly and gave J3 a simple set of instructions.

He said, "This won't take long. Mr. Cordova just wants to show you, his gratitude. You can take it or leave it. It's your choice. But for now, let's go."

As J3 began to exit the vehicle I grabbed my door handle to exit as well. Then the Colombian tapped me on my shoulder and said, "No, not you. You stay put."

As J3 closed his door, the Colombian slid over to the driver side passenger door and exited from the driver side behind him. I watched as J3 walked toward the men in front of him and then out of nowhere I heard a loud bang.

Then I watched in horror as J3's body quickly fell to the ground. The Colombian who had been riding with us in the back seat casually walked up behind J3 and shot him in the back of his head. And just like that, J3 was dead. It happened so fast that he never saw it coming.

187

As J3 lay dead on the ground the men in front of him immediately opened their suitcases that they placed on the hood of his car. Inside their suitcases wasn't money, but cleaning materials. One suitcase had a large plastic tarp mat and a small bag of lye. And the other suitcase had a box of gloves and several cleaning supplies.

I watched in fear as they unwrapped the tarp and prepared to roll J3's body in it. All three men put on gloves and then placed gowns over their tops. They were quiet and moved quickly. They didn't say a word to each other, and they moved about as if they were doing something they had done many times before.

While watching these men my heart beat feverishly. I was afraid but I dared not make a sudden move or make even the slightest sound. I just stared ahead and watched. And as I watched, I hoped and prayed that I wouldn't be next. I tried my best to remain invisible.

But I knew they saw me, and I hoped and prayed they wouldn't interact with me. I hoped and prayed they wouldn't motion for me to get out. The thought of getting out of the car made me tremble with fear. I was afraid and completely powerless. The only thing I could do was watch them as they worked in precision and complete unison.

I watched as they rolled J3's body onto the mat. One of the men grabbed J3's legs, then another grabbed his torso. Then the third man grabbed his head and shoulders. Then all three of them hurriedly carried J3's body into the woods and disappeared into the night. They were quiet, calm, and unbothered by what they had just done.

When they reappeared from the woods two of the men took off their gloves and gowns and placed them in a large plastic bag. The third man, the one who sat in the back seat, grabbed a bag of lye from the hood of the car and walked back into the woods. I knew what the lye was for. It

188

was used to prevent the body from releasing a deteriorating smell that would attract large birds and buzzards or catch the nose of anyone close by or anyone parked in the area.

After the man reappeared from the woods, he took off his gloves and gown then balled them up and placed them in the large trash bag. Then he took the garbage bag and twisted it up and threw it in the back of the trunk of the car in front of me. Then another one of the other men took out a container of what appeared to be bleach and poured it on the ground at the spot where J3's body fell.

I couldn't see what he was doing but I could hear the liquid as it poured to the ground. When he finished the man tossed the empty container in the back of the truck and closed it shut. He then walked to the front of the car and took a seat in the driver seat. The two other men talked briefly before one of them went and took a seat in the front passenger seat of the vehicle.

Then the Columbian man who rode with me and J3 approached me. He walked over to the passenger side door where I was sitting, grabbed the door handle and opened it, and then he gave me my final orders.

He said, "You have done a good deed. You are a man to whom my country will be forever grateful. You are definitely a tough guy. Someone who I respect. Take these items and do whatever you must with them."

The man then handed me J3's car keys, his wallet, a ring, and his cellphone.

He said, "We are done here. After you drive yourself back to your hotel, get rid of this car. Wipe it down for prints and ditch it. You can park it wherever you like but when you walk away from it, never go back. Bad things happen when we walk backwards."

He then handed me a business card. The card was for a mechanic named Carlos. He said if I ever need him for

189

anything I should contact Carlos and he would know how to reach him.

Then he pulled a white cloth from his back pocket and opened the rear passenger door. He wiped down the outside and inside door handle and also the seat where he sat. Then he walked to the driver side passenger door and did the same thing over there. Then he looked at me, nodded his head and sat in the car in front of me. Then they drove off.

After they drove away, I moved to the driver's seat, put the keys in the ignition and slowly started to drive away. As I drove, I looked in the rear-view mirror toward the area of the woods where they took J3's body and a sudden chill moved across the back of my neck. I quickly put my foot on the gas pedal and drove away and never looked back again.

I made my way to the main road and headed back to the hotel to get my things. I needed to get to my car and get out of J3's vehicle as soon as possible. I was nervous about what just happened, but I felt relieved to have J3 finally out of the picture. It was a good feeling. I had done what I set out to do and now I could focus on Diana and being a part of her life.

J3 meant nothing to me and the thought of what happened a few miles back garnered no energy or emotions from me. I was confident I had done the right thing. Removing him from the picture made things easier. My head felt lighter, and my mind was clearer.

As I drove back to the hotel, I realized I never really had a plan for dealing with J3, but I always believed everything would fall into place. The conversations I had with the Columbians, the conversations I had with Diana and even the short conversations I had with J3, none of them were planned. Yet things seemed to fall into place.

And even though I hadn't officially planned my next move I felt good and confident that it too would fall into place. While driving down the road I started looking at the things that the Colombian gave me in the parking lot.

First, I analyzed the wallet. When I looked at his driver's license, I found out his name was Calvin Lawrence, and it was amazing how much we resembled each other. The smile on his ID picture was almost identical to the way I smiled on mine. His height and weight and eye color were all very similar to mine.

We were by most accounts' exact replicas of one another. So much so that Diana and her son couldn't tell me from him when I met them at the library. Even the facial scanner the deputies used at the hotel couldn't tell us apart. I knew our similarities would be something I would probably never get an answer to, but at this point it wasn't something I was concerned about.

Then I reached into my pocket and pulled out the other item the Colombian handed me. It was a ring. I hoped it wasn't a wedding or engagement ring because that would really complicate things. But to my surprise it was just a basic ring. Just a cheap ordinary ring. It was nothing spectacular, so I let down the window and threw it away.

Then I grabbed J3's cell phone. It was clearly dead because when I tried to power it on nothing happened. It hadn't been charged in the two weeks he was at trial. I couldn't turn it on, but I knew I needed to hold on to it because his contacts might provide clues down the road into his life and who he was.

Maybe they would reveal the answers to why we strongly resembled each other. I knew it might be useful, so I put his phone in my front pocket and continued driving down the road. Before no time I was nearing my destination.

191

It was almost 9:30 p.m. and I had just driven by the courthouse.

Like usual there were a bunch of cars parked around the perimeter and people were standing around doing nothing. They were still there even at this late hour. I wondered what the news was now that it had been almost two hours since the jury failed to convict Mr. Cordova. There were so many people out there that it was obvious the verdict was still fresh on people's minds.

As I passed by the courthouse I glanced over at the entrance. The same entrance I had lined up in front of at 6:30 in the morning to make sure I got a good seat at the trial. It was also the same line that the Colombian men had lined up in as well.

Then I remembered what the Colombian told me before we parted ways. When he handed me J3's car keys, wallet, cell phone and ring he told me those things meant nothing to him and for me to do with them whatever I wanted. At first it didn't register to me what those words meant. But now those words were ringing loud and clear.

I had J3's car, his car keys, his wallet with his driver's license and his cell phone. I had everything I needed to be him. I had what I needed for me to get close to Diana. My goals were all right in front of me.

It made sense for me to keep these things because in order for me to get close to Diana I had to appear to be him. I had done it once before at the library and I was sure I could do it again. Instead of ditching his car I would keep it and ditch mine. Not permanently. Just long enough until I figured all of this out.

But I didn't know where to ditch it or park it. Maybe I would park it at the mall. Or maybe a local grocery store. Or maybe at a busy hotel. I had so many choices.

And because this was a small town, I knew wherever I parked it I had to make sure I didn't draw any attention. If I did, my car would be towed, and I didn't need the headache of that. As I neared my hotel, I happened to drive past a large apartment complex.

It had plenty of parking spaces and surely no one would mind if I parked my car in one of them. So that's what I planned. It was the perfect spot for me to park my car and not bring any attention to myself.

When I pulled into the hotel parking lot, I jumped out of J3's car and into mine. Then I drove a mile up the road to the apartment complex and parked my car. It was dark outside and there was no one moving about in the parking lot.

I parked my car and was confident it would be there when I returned. So, after I parked it, I turned around and walked the mile or so back to my hotel. When I returned to my room it was almost 11:00 p.m.

I decided it made the most sense for me to leave in the morning and then hit the road to see Diana. When I laid back on the bed and thought about everything that happened today, I felt empowered and more confident than ever. I was close to making my dream a reality. Luck was on my side. I couldn't wait for tomorrow and what it would bring.

The next morning, I loaded up my suitcase and cleaned out my hotel room. I threw away all the food and snacks the Colombians had bought for me and left my room as clean as it was when I entered it. When I grabbed my suitcase off the floor, I looked around one more time then I closed the door on this short chapter of my life.

When I opened the trunk to put my suitcase in it, to my surprise there was already a suitcase inside. It was J3's suitcase. I knew it wouldn't be necessary for me to have two suitcases, so I left his suitcase there and threw my suitcase in the nearest dumpster. For the next couple days, I was gonna be him so why not wear his clothes and keep his stuff. It only made sense.

Now I was officially ready to hit the road and start my two-hour drive to Diana's home. When I put the key in the ignition and started down the highway, I was relieved. I couldn't believe I was heading back to see her. The woman of my dreams.

After a few minutes on the road, I started preparing myself for what would happen when I laid eyes on her again. I wondered what questions she would ask me. I was sure she would want to know about the trial.

It was the biggest news in the country. And I was also sure that she would have heard that there was a mistrial and that Mr. Cordova had been set free. Then more questions ran through my head.

Like what would I say if she asks me why I didn't call her at the conclusion of the trial. Yes, my phone was dead, but I had all night to charge it up. How could I answer that? Why would a dead phone stop me from calling her?

I could have easily left my room and used the hotel phone. I didn't really have an answer to that. Not yet. And I knew I needed answers to that question and a slew of others.

Like the questions regarding their relationship. I didn't know how close or involved they were. That was by far the most difficult hurdle I had to overcome. When we eventually meet up, the only thing I can do is try to read her body language and take things slow.

I had to take my time with this. If I rushed, it would be a foolish mistake. One I couldn't afford to make.

I figured that would be the trickiest part of me popping up in her life appearing to be someone I was not. I knew I would have to somehow get her to like me for who I am not who she thought I was. That would be my biggest challenge.

Aside from those questions, many of the questions I had were the same ones I had when I prepared to meet her at the library. And surprisingly, everything went very smoothly. She couldn't tell me from J3, and she welcomed me.

And before I left, she gave me a hug and told me she would miss me while I was gone. I was confident this would work out. She didn't suspect anything then, and I doubted she would suspect anything now. But I knew this time things would be different. I wasn't going to meet her at the library. I was meeting her at her home.

Chapter 23

Second Chances

I was going to knock on her door at 910 Blue heart Lane and step right in as if I was J3. This was totally different from the meeting at the library. This was way deeper than that. This time I had zero margin for error.

What I was doing was not only dangerous, but it was morally wrong. I was planning to be an imposter. There was no good way to spin it. I had to take my time and do this right.

And once again my biggest worry was that she would ask me a bunch of questions I didn't have answers to because I had zero chance of answering even the most basic of questions. There was no way I could answer them. I didn't know how this was gonna play out.

And as much as I wanted to feel and appear confident, I couldn't because there was so much about her I didn't know. And that really bothered me. I had fallen in love with a woman who I really didn't know much about.

How could I get around that? I had to come up with something. I needed some type of way to justify having a slight memory loss. Something that would buy me a little time and give me a reason for not remembering certain things that I should. As strange as it sounded, I realized I needed to be in an accident.

I needed to be in an accident that wouldn't harm me but would give the impression that I had been injured. A car accident would do just the trick. An accident that made me appear injured but without any physical injuries.

I loved the way it sounded, and I couldn't believe I had come up with this plan. It was masterful. It was the perfect answer to solve my problems. Diana couldn't expect me to remember things if I had amnesia or if I had a concussion from a small car accident.

I was only about thirty minutes from her home and was driving down a long country road. If only a deer would shoot across the road and force me to hit it. That would simplify things for me. That would be my accident.

But I knew that would never happen. The chances of a deer popping in front of me when I wanted it were nearly impossible. That's when I decided that the easiest way to pull this off would be to create the accident myself. All I had to do was drive into a tree and slightly damage the front end of the vehicle.

That would damage the car but wouldn't hurt me. I liked the way that sounded so that was my plan. I pulled off the main road and drove down a smaller, more isolated road. Then I found a small tree that was strong enough to withstand a minor collision and drove the driver side of J3's vehicle right smack into it.

I didn't drive into it very hard, just hard enough to create a nice sized dent.
I would tell Diana that I swerved off the road to avoid hitting a deer and hit a tree. And that would be my excuse for not remembering things. I would tell her I had a headache and maybe a slight concussion.

Not only was this excuse believable but it was masterful. I was proud of myself. I couldn't believe I came up with this.

Not knowing what to expect and not being prepared had unfortunately been my calling card. Every step along this journey had been a gamble and I had won. But in spite of how confident I was, there was still a lot of uncertainty with what I was attempting to do.

I really didn't know what to expect from Diana. All I could do was hope for the best. And after I damaged the front end of J3's vehicle, the drive to Diana's home was a short one. Within no time I was near her doorstep.

It had taken me a little over two hours from the time I left Jefferson County to the time I arrived at her home. And those two hours zoomed by fast.

It seemed like days ago that I watched J3's execution. But in fact, it had only been a couple of hours ago. I put that incident so far behind me that it seemed like a distant memory.

As I neared Diana's home, I tried to prepare myself for what might happen when she answered the door. I hadn't seen her in eleven days. The last time I saw her was at the library on the Wednesday before I left for the trial. Today was Saturday.

Eleven days had passed, and I had been away for almost two weeks. She told me she would miss me while I was gone so I anticipated a warm welcome and a showering of kind words. As I pulled up to Diana's home, I put J3's wallet and cell phone in my pocket then I took my wallet and placed it under the floor mat under the driver's seat.

I had to make sure I had all the small things I needed to make this work. When I turned off the car I took a few minutes, sat in the driver's seat, and tried to process what was going on. I tried to process the situation I was getting ready to walk into. There were so many things that could go wrong with what I was doing.

I was essentially preparing myself to be someone else. My plan was to try to make Diana think that I was J3 and then work my way into her life. It was risky and definitely not something I had spent a lot of time preparing for. And as bad as I wanted to believe everything would work out, I had an odd feeling that it wouldn't.

Something just felt wrong about what I was doing. I was readying myself to play mind games with her and I knew that wasn't cool. But it was the only option I had. There was no other way I could make this work. So I had to give it a try. I had done too much to turn back now.

As I sat in the car meditating and thinking about my next step, to my surprise the door to Diana's home opened and out she came. She was walking right toward me. I didn't have a chance to do anything but get out of the car and greet her.

As soon as I stepped out, she was standing right in front of me surveying the damage to the front of the car. She said, "Oh my God Calvin, what happened to your car? Were you in an accident?"

I said, "Yeah, I was. I had a dang on a deer run across the road. I swerved to keep from hitting him and wound up hitting a tree off the side of the road."
Diana said, "Oh my goodness. Are you okay?"

I said, "I'm okay. I just have this massive headache and feel a little dizzy. But I'm okay. I think I just need to rest."

Then she said, "Well come inside. Let's talk about it."
I told her, "Thank you. I really appreciate it."

Diana was now holding my hand and escorting me toward her house. Once inside she walked me to the couch, and I took a seat. And that's when the barrage of questions came. The questions I had hoped to avoid by creating my self-inflicted car accident.

She said, "So where did you have this accident, and how long have you been driving with your car damaged like that?"

199

I said, "It wasn't that long. Maybe ten or fifteen miles back. I was turning off the main road and he was on the shoulder. He just ran out in front of me."

She said, "Well you might need to go to the hospital. You could have a concussion."

I said, "I'm okay. If this headache doesn't go away in a few hours, I'll go. But for now, I'm good."

Then she said, "Okay. Well, I'm glad you're back. We have a lot to talk about. But first, why didn't you call me? I saw on the news the trial ended last night. I wanted to talk to you. You didn't call me last night or this morning. What's up with that?"

I said, "I'm sorry. When the trial ended, they gave us back our phones but mine was dead and I didn't have my charger. I must have left it at home. Then when I went back to the hotel, I was only planning on taking a quick nap but by the time I woke up it was morning. So, I just decided to head on back. So yeah, I'm sorry I didn't call you. But I'm here now."

Diana said, "So you were so tired that you couldn't go get a charger and call me?"
I said, "Yeah, I was. That trial was something else. It was draining."

She replied, "I bet. So how in the world could you guys not come up with a verdict? That man is guilty. That's all everybody's been talking about. They said on the news that one of the jurors may have sabotaged the trial. They didn't say the name of the juror, but they say the FBI is looking into it. It's been all over the news. They think someone may have paid one of the jurors."

I said, "Wow, that's crazy. I don't know anything about that. I haven't watched any of the news so I'm not sure what they're talking about. And I kinda don't really wanna talk about that right now. That case was long and draining.

200

And for it to end like it did, well that was something else. And right now, my head is banging."

Diana interrupted and asked, "Are you sure you don't wanna go to the hospital and have it looked at?"

I said, "Yes, I'm sure."

Then she asked, "So how long were you parked outside? I just happened to look out the window and saw your car parked. I saw you just sitting there. I thought you were asleep. You were sitting out there with your eyes closed."

I replied back, "Yeah, I was just resting. At one point when I was sitting there, I couldn't remember what house you lived in. I wasn't sure if I was at the right house. So I just sat there, and I closed my eyes and tried to remember which house was yours. And then you came out. I don't even remember how I got here. Only thing I remember is parking in front of your house and just sitting there."

Then Diana said, "Well I'm glad you made it safely. It sounds like you have a mild concussion. If you don't remember things that's not good. You can sit here and rest but don't get too comfortable. We have some other things to talk about."

At this point I was feeling pretty good about how things were playing out. I had obviously convinced Diana that I was Calvin. I had convinced her that I had been in an accident and that my mind was a little fuzzy.

I had bought myself some time and hoped she wouldn't ask me a bunch more questions. Overall, I felt good with how things were going. And I was pleased that Diana seemed to have a genuine concern about my wellbeing.

But I was also puzzled by her lack of intimacy toward me. We didn't hug, kiss, cuddle or anything I had expected. When she walked outside to greet me, after she finished asking questions about the damage to the car, she grabbed my arm and helped me inside.

Then once inside she helped me to a seat on her couch and then she sat across from me. She sat on the opposite couch. There was no physical interaction between us at all. None. Not even a hug.

Diana was kind, helpful and very talkative but I could feel something was missing. If someone you cared about had been away from you for almost two weeks, I would think the first thing you would do when you saw that person would be to give them a hug. You would give them a big hug. But she didn't.

And when she sat away from me on the couch I wondered why. Why didn't she sit next to me? I was picking up on things that I wished I hadn't. Then I homed in on something else she said. When Diana said for me to sit here and rest but don't get too comfortable because we have things to talk about, well I knew that was not good. I felt as if I was in trouble. I felt like I had done something wrong.

After a few more minutes of small talk the conversation I dreaded came. Diane started the second phase of our conversation by asking me again if I was feeling any better. I told her I was but that I still had a small headache. And as much as I hinted about having a headache, she still proceeded to tell me what was on her mind.

And unfortunately for me she had a bunch of things on her mind. And as she spoke, I couldn't do anything but listen. And what I heard caught me completely off guard.

She said, "Well, I hate that you're not feeling well but like I said earlier I'm glad you are okay. Do you remember the conversation we had before you left?"

I said, "No. Not really."

She said, "We talked about several things. It was the Monday before you left for the trial. Do you remember our conversation Monday morning?"

I said, "No," while shaking my head in confusion.

Diana said, "Well let me help you. We talked about giving each other space. Do you remember that?"

I replied, "I'm sorry Diana. I don't remember. I think the accident may have something to do with it. I could barely remember how I got here. What do you mean by giving each other space? I don't remember. What did we discuss?"

Diana said, "We talked about how I think you are an amazing man but I'm not feeling you like I think you're feeling me. I told you I felt there was something about this relationship that seemed odd and no matter how many times I try to make sense of it I don't see you as anything other than a friend. Do you remember us talking about that?"

I said, "No, I'm sorry but I don't remember."

She said, "Well we did. And you said you understood and would respect my wishes. We both agreed to slow things down. Do you remember that?"

I said, "No. I'm sorry. I don't remember any of this. But I'm listening."

Then Diana said, "Okay. Good. Well after we talked, the next day I got the card in the mail from you. The card that said you had jury duty and would be away for a while. I thought the card was nice. It was a sweet card. At the bottom of the card, you said you would talk to me when you get back in two weeks."

"Then the very next day you showed up at the library. Now that really had me confused. You said you wanted to see me before you left. I didn't say anything then because I had my son with me but that really had me concerned.

"I couldn't understand why you came to the library after we had just talked a few days before about giving each

203

other space. It was almost like you didn't care about what we discussed. I felt like you blew off my concerns when you showed up like that.

"The library is my private time. That's the time I set aside for me and my son. And I told you that. I really wasn't okay with you showing up like you did."

I replied back, "I'm sorry Diana. I had a lot going on at the time. I wish I could tell you everything but… I can't explain it."

She said, "Well I'm not done. So the library incident was one thing. But then when I got home, I looked at my security camera. And that's when I knew that this thing, this whatever you wanna call it. This is over! I saw you, Calvin. I saw you in my home!

"You were snooping around and looking through my mail. Taking pictures of my things. That was crazy! What were you thinking? Are you that obsessed with me? I can't believe you broke into my home.

"I only walked you in here so I could tell you face to face to leave me and my son alone. I don't feel safe around you anymore. I want you to leave. After today I don't want you coming around here anymore. Not tomorrow. Not next week. Not ever.

"And please, please don't follow me and my son. And don't ever show up at the library again. I don't want you around us anymore. I'm raising him to be a good man and no good man breaks into a woman's home and snoops around her things.

"From day one I told you I liked you but nothing more than that. And now I see why. What were you thinking, Calvin? Why would you do that?"

Diana was angry and she had tears in her eyes. She was truly upset and disappointed in my actions. At this point

I didn't know what to say. I was just as shocked to hear what she told me as she was to tell me.

I couldn't believe how bad things had gone and I knew my time here was up. There was nothing I could do to save this conversation. I had violated her trust and she wasn't safe around me anymore. It was time for me to go. As much as I wanted to make this work, I had no answers to what she just told me. I knew I had to go.

I said, "I don't know what I was thinking. I can't explain it. And you're right, I think it's best if I leave."

Diana said, "I think so too. And this time please respect my wishes. Please leave me and my son alone and let us be. I haven't reported your break-in to the police, but I have the video. If you come around here again, ever again, I'm going to the police."

I said, "I understand. You won't hear from me again. I promise. I'm really sorry about everything and I wish I could explain it, but I can't."

And just like that... we were done. The woman of my dreams had officially cut me loose. She was done with me and there was nothing I could do about it. For all the planning I did, I failed to plan for her having a security camera at her home. I never once thought about it. Not once.

My poor planning had done me in. And now I was a miserable man. When I gathered myself and left her home a sudden emptiness filled me. When she walked me to the door, I didn't even look back at her to say goodbye. I had failed. I had failed miserably. Everything I had done; I did for her. Everywhere I went, I went for her.

And now with her out of the picture I felt a sense of worthlessness. The only thing left for me to do now was to head back to Jefferson County and get my car and then go back home.

Chapter 24

Going Home

I had already wrecked J3's car so driving it two hours away was not an option. I had to ditch it and catch a ride back to get mine. So I drove his car to an abandoned field about two miles off the main road and I parked it there. Then I took his suitcase out the trunk and made the twenty-minute walk to the main road.

That was the longest walk I had taken in a long time. Not only was it hot and humid outside but J3's suitcase was heavier than I thought. It didn't have any wheels at the bottom, so I had to carry it the whole way.

And after a mile or so I got tired of carrying it, so I tossed it into the brushes on the side of the road and kept walking. Then I reached in my front pocket and took out J3's wallet and tossed that in the bushes as well. Then I tossed away his cell phone.

None of those things were worth me carrying around anymore. And it felt good tossing his things away. I didn't need them anymore. And when I reached the main road, I felt even better.

I just wanted to get to my car and head back home. Though my home was simple, and my life was unflattering, I longed for them both. Once I got to the main road, I walked to the nearest gas station which was another mile away.

While there I got directions to the nearest bus station which I was told was about ten miles away. So then I caught a cab there and took a Greyhound bus back to

Jefferson County. The bus ride was long and quiet. There couldn't have been more than ten people on the bus, and for the most part it seemed like everyone on the bus except me was asleep.

I wished I could have taken a nap, but I couldn't. The whole ride there I hoped my car was in the same place where I parked it. Even though I hadn't left it there long, it was parked in an apartment complex. All it would take was one nosey neighbor's complaint that I had parked in their space and then my car would be towed. So that's all I thought about on the bus ride.

After a few hours, the bus pulled into the Greyhound Station in Jefferson County. I didn't know the name of the apartment complex where I parked my car, but I knew it was a short walk from the hotel I had stayed in for almost a week. So I took a cab back to the hotel.

Never in my wildest dreams could I have imagined I would be back at this hotel so soon. But here I was, pulling into the hotel parking lot one more time.

When the cab pulled into the main parking lot there was a large police presence and several news trucks broadcasting from in front of the hotel's office. It was clear that something big had happened. I was curious to know what was going on, but I didn't stop to ask anybody any questions. I had to get my car back before it got towed.

When I got out of the cab, I didn't waste any time. I started walking down the street to the apartment complex to get my car. And to my relief my car was exactly where I left it. I got in, turned the key and was officially on my way back home.

I was going back home to the life I had lived just a few weeks prior. A life that was simple and easy and free of stress. These last two weeks had taken a toll on me, and it seemed like I was gone for an eternity. It felt good to be on the road heading home.

When I arrived at my home I sat on the couch and felt a major relief. I had been far away from home, and it felt good to be sitting on my couch in the comforts of my home. Everything in my apartment was exactly how I left it and my quiet uneventful life had welcomed me back.

While sitting on the couch relaxing it felt at times like I had never left. But I did. And I would never forget the things I had done and the people I met. And in spite of everything that had gone wrong, I didn't regret much.

I had no remorse about what happened to J3, and I had no ill feelings toward Diana. What happened, and in my mind, I would have done everything all over again for her love.

A love that J3 took for granted. He had mismanaged the most important person in his life. He betrayed his commitment to Diana by flirting with the young juror. And before I came into the picture, he had already done things that made Diana take a pause from him.

So he was a loser. With him the chips fell where they did and, in the end, he was a casualty of his own failures. I had no sympathy for him.

While sitting on the couch I grabbed the remote and turned the TV to the news. The case of the Colombian was still being covered. The reporter was talking about how the trial had spiraled into one of national attention and how the government was completely caught off guard by the verdict. The reporter said the government has knowledge that Colombian agents may have influenced this trial.

He said there was also a nationwide manhunt for one of the jurors who had gone missing. He described the juror as possibly being responsible or involved in the mistrial. He said the missing juror helped to undermine the judicial process and may have taken a bribe. He said the juror may have been involved with Colombian agents.

While he spoke, a picture of J3 popped up in the background. The reporter called him by his name… Calvin Lawrence. He said that Calvin's picture was being shown to networks all over the country and there was a nationwide manhunt to find him.

Then the reporter said federal agents had gone to the home of a female friend of Calvin's and that she reported seeing Calvin recently. The reporter said Calvin's female friend said he had been acting very strange and that she asked him to stay away from her and her son.

Then the reporter said FBI agents had reported finding Calvin's car abandoned along a county road not far from the home of his female friend. A wallet, cell phone and other forms of identification belonging to Calvin were also found in the area near where they found his car. The reporter said for anyone with information about Calvin Lawrence's whereabouts was to call the FBI at the number he provided.

I couldn't believe what I just saw. Calvin was reported missing and had officially become one of the FBI's most wanted persons. Had he been alive he would be in a world of trouble. But Calvin was dead, and I knew at some point they would find him.

And seeing Calvin's picture on the news made me nervous. I thought it would be only a matter of time before the agents found Calvin's deceased body in the woods behind those industrial warehouses. And when they found him, I imagined all hell would break loose.

It was at this moment that I felt remorse for what I had done. I felt bad for what I had orchestrated. I felt grief that I had allowed myself to be a part of a plot to acquit a dangerous man who preyed on the weak. So many terrible things were happening all around me.

But I didn't feel bad for Calvin, I felt bad for Diana. I felt terrible when I thought about what she must be feeling. She was suddenly right smack in the middle of Calvin's mess. And because he had gone missing, I was sure she had all types of agents stationed around her home, asking her personal questions, and putting her life through a microscope.

I felt bad for her. She didn't deserve any of this. She was still in my heart, and I felt like I had crushed it twice. And as much as I wanted to do something, I knew there was nothing I could do.

I refused to let the drama of J3 consume me. I had to get on with my life. I needed to get back to my routine. Tomorrow I would call my employer and tell them I was returning to work. Weeks ago, I told them I was taking time off to be with an ill family member.

But now it was time for me to resume the life I had made for myself. So tomorrow I would call them and let them know I was ready to return to work. But going back to work would be an even bigger problem than the problems I already created. As a journalist, I knew that when I went back my employer would almost certainly want me to cover the story of the Colombian and the missing juror.

And I also knew that there was a strong possibility that they would expect me to go back to the same town I just left. They would almost certainly send me back to Jefferson County to cover the story that I had helped create. And I wanted no part of going back there.

I wondered how I could avoid it. How could I be expected to cover a story about a mistrial I had helped to corrupt? I couldn't do it. How could I tell my boss that I wanted no part of the biggest story in the country?

Over the years my career had taken off. I rose from a small-time writer covering local news to a major well-known journalist who covered the top stories from all over the country. I was one of the lead reporters for the Atlanta Journal-Constitution.

I knew that, not only would my employer expect me to cover the case, but they would expect me to make arrangements to interview all the players. That's what I did. For every story I covered, I interviewed all the major players.

I interviewed the lawyers, the prosecutors, the politicians, the family members, the victims, and the accused. I interviewed everyone. And I was good at what I did. I followed every lead. I left no stone unturned.

My reporting was second to none. But if I was assigned this case, I would almost certainly be expected to interview the major players. And one of those players would be Diana. She was the missing juror's female friend. His car was found not far from her home.

Interviewing her would be something my employer would expect me to do, but something I knew I couldn't. It would be an impossible assignment. I had to figure a way out. There was no way I could take on this assignment. I needed to think of something. I had to avoid that assignment at all costs.

Chapter 25

A Call from Mama

While I was pondering my next move, I received a welcoming yet unexpected phone call from my mother. I had not talked to her since I made my trip to see Diana.

On most occasions I would call her at least once a week to check in. But I had been so preoccupied with Diana that I hadn't called her or even checked my voicemail for the messages she left me.

She said she called me twice since I was gone but didn't leave a message. She said she initially just called me to say hello, but this call was different. This would be a completely different conversation than the one my mother planned for me a few days ago.

Different from any other conversation we had ever had before. When I answered the phone, I could almost immediately tell that something was wrong. The cheerful and enthusiastic voice that always greeted me had been altered. I could sense a worried tone in her voice.

After my somewhat fake, half-exciting greeting of, "Hello mom! How are you?" Her response was noticeably one of a mellowed-out concern.

My mother said, "I'm good, son. How are you? I called you a couple of times, but you haven't returned any of my calls. Is everything okay? I've been worried about you."

I said, "I'm fine mom. Everything is fine. I haven't had a chance to check my voicemail in a while because I've been busy with work. Is everything okay? You seem a little down."

She said, "Well actually it's not okay. I don't know how to tell you this, but I just had a visit with two police officers. They were FBI agents. And they were asking me all types of questions about you. They asked me a lot of stuff… I'm worried about you son."

I replied, "Agents? FBI agents? Why on Earth would agents be asking you questions about me? Are you sure they were from the FBI?"

She said, "Yes. I'm sure. They had their badges, their guns, and IDs. And they gave me their business cards with their contact information. And when they left, I called the numbers on their cards and they were legit. They say you may be in some type of trouble. They say you may be in danger."

I said, "they said I might be in danger, danger from what? And what did they mean I might be in some type of trouble. I haven't done anything. What on Earth were they talking about?"

At this point I was genuinely concerned that the FBI was looking for me. In my mind I had done nothing wrong. On the news they said they were looking for Calvin. They made no mention of me. For all they knew I was invisible. No one knew anything about me.

Other than J3 and the Colombians I hadn't spoken to anyone. I was confident that the FBI was on the wrong trail. My voice over the phone was one of confidence and I tried to assure my mother that everything was fine, but my mother knew better. She was the one person who knew me best. She wasn't buying it. Something was wrong and she wanted me to know she knew it.

My mother said, "Well they asked me if I knew where you were and when was the last time I talked to you. I told them I hadn't spoken to you in about two weeks, and I didn't know where you were. Then they asked me where you lived and where you worked. Then they asked me for your phone number.

"At first, I didn't answer any of their questions. I was scared and I didn't know what they wanted. But when they told me your life might be in danger, well that's when I opened up and talked to them. That's when I told them what I knew.

"And even though they asked me where you worked, they already knew it. They had already talked to your boss before they came to see me. They had a copy of your emergency contact card from work with them.

"You listed my name and address as a contact in case of an emergency. So when they showed me that I knew they were serious. They had already done their research. I knew these people weren't playing."

I said, "Okay. So, did they say why they went to my job? And why would my job give them my emergency contact info. Why do they need that?"

She said, "they say you took off work for a few weeks to go and visit a sick family member. Your job said they haven't heard from you since you left two weeks ago. And then the agent says someone from your job called them after they saw something on the news that startled them.

"The person from your job called them and said that the missing juror everyone's been looking for looked a lot like you. So they asked the FBI to look into it. Are you familiar with the story on the news about the missing juror?"

I said, "Yeah, I heard a little bit about it. So they say someone called them because I looked like someone they saw on TV. Well, that's a first."

She said, "The agents say they called you. They say they left you messages, but you haven't responded to their

215

calls. And yes, the missing juror does look a lot like you. His face has been on every channel all over the country. All day. All they show is his face. That man is a wanted man."

I said, "So they are looking for me because someone on television looks like me. What crime is that? There are six billion people on this planet. We're bound to have someone we look like floating around out there."

My sarcasm was immediately interrupted by a firm and stern voice from my mother.

She said, "Curtis! Enough. That's enough! These people aren't playing. They say you were at that trial. They say you may be responsible for helping that man get off. And they have evidence against you.

"They showed me a video of you sitting in the courtroom. I saw it. It was you. You were sitting there with a wig on, and you also had on a fake mustache and glasses. I saw the video.

"They say you were there every day. Every day you were there taking notes. They say you were taking notes on people in the jury. Son, is this true? These people say your life may be in danger."

I may have been a lot of things but one thing I wasn't was a liar. I couldn't lie to my mother. She was all I had. If I violated her trust, there was no one else out there I could turn to. I wanted to tell her the truth, but I couldn't. I couldn't tell her the whole truth so I told her as much of the truth as I could.

I said, "Yes mama. I was there. I was there because I'm a journalist. I'm a reporter. That's what I do. It's what I'm good at. I was there to get the inside scoop on the biggest corruption case in this country in over half a century.

"Mr. Cordova claimed he had proof that members of Congress were involved in his international sex ring. And

216

that was a big accusation. Every good reporter wanted a piece of that story. So yes, I was there.

"But I wasn't there because of my job. I was there because I wanted to get the scoop on my own. That's why I didn't tell my job where I was."

My mother interrupted me and said, "So if you weren't there for work why were you there? Your job said they haven't heard from you in over two weeks. And why did you tell them you had to go visit a sick family member? We don't have nobody sick in our family."

I said, "I just told them that so I could get away and cover the story like a private citizen. I didn't wanna be working and sending information to them every day. I was on my own. I just wanted to go and take in the whole trial on my own. On my own time and on my own dime. I didn't want to do it for them. I went there for myself."

At this point I actually started to believe the lie I had been telling my mother. It not only made sense, but it was believable. I had suddenly become pretty good at making stuff up. I had done it with the Colombians when they came into my room.

When they held a gun to me and asked me who I was and why I was there. At only a moment's notice I came up with a story that I was there to prevent J3 from inheriting my grandmother's money. And the Colombians believed it and they sympathized with me.

So I thought my mother was on board as well. I thought my story was going great. I was quick on my feet and came up with a brilliant excuse. I thought she believed me. But not my mother. She wasn't buying it. She didn't believe any part of it.

Chapter 26

A Time to Listen

My mother became frustrated and responded, "Listen Curtis! I don't wanna hear all this nonsense. Cause you and I both know that's a lie. I've always told you I got your back when you're right. But when you're wrong you need to own up to it. I will not support or tolerate a liar. I won't do it!"

At this point I was silent on the other end of the phone. I had lied to my mother and that was one thing I never did. I never had to. I was never in a situation where I needed to.

When my father died, she raised me and my sister as best she could. She raised us to love and respect each other. And growing up we were all we had, and we learned early on that we had to trust each other. And here I was violating her trust.

I couldn't lie anymore. I told myself I wouldn't lie anymore. So I just sat quietly on the other end of the phone. My silence was my admitting that I had lied, and it gave my mother a green light to take charge of the conversation. She had my full attention. I wasn't lying anymore. This was a time to listen.

She said, "The agents didn't just have a video of you at the courthouse. They have lots of videos of you. And they showed me other videos. They have a video of you at the same hotel where the jurors were staying.

They showed me a video of you going in the hotel with that same disguise that you had on in court. It shows you walking through the lobby and then it shows you going to the bathroom. You were there for a long time.

Then you came out of the bathroom and went to the room of the missing juror. They got it all on video. They say you were alone in his room for almost thirty minutes before he came back from breakfast.

Then y'all was in there together. Then the video shows him leaving the room to go to the courthouse with the other jurors. But you didn't leave that room for almost another hour. You stayed in his room until all the police left the hotel.

And after they left, that's when you left. The video shows you going out the back exit. I saw it. I saw all of it. That's why I'm worried about you. You done got yourself in a whole lot of mess."

Hearing all of this I could do nothing but remain silent and listen. My mother was the wisest person I knew. There was nothing I could do or say to justify the things she called me out on. I was trapped by my own lies.

I had no idea they had a video of me at J3's hotel. I never once thought about the possibility of being caught on video. It never crossed my mind. First, I was caught by Diana's home security and now I was caught by J3's hotel security. Once again, my lack of planning was on full display.

Hearing that the FBI knew so much about me and my movements definitely made me worry. I couldn't understand how they had pieced it all together. How did they zero in on me and how did they do it so quickly?

The trial had just ended yesterday, and they were hot on my trail. I figured when one of my coworkers called the FBI that's what got the ball rolling. That one phone call must have opened the door for them to focus on me. In my mind I pieced together how things must have played out:

1. One of my coworkers calls the FBI letting them know that the missing juror looked a lot like me.
2. The FBI pays my job a visit.
3. My boss tells them I haven't been to work in two weeks. He tells them I requested leave to spend time with a sick family member.
4. My leave just happens to be during the two-week window of the trial.
5. FBI agents review video from the courthouse and see me in disguise every day.
6. The one day I didn't go to court was when I went to J3's hotel.
7. They review the video and see me enter the hotel lobby, then go into the bathroom. Then they see me enter his room while he's at breakfast. Then they watched a video of me leaving the hotel after all the police had left.
8. The FBI showed up at my hotel in Jefferson County, but I had already checked out.
9. Agents take the hotel video to my mother who is listed as my emergency contact.
10. My mother verifies that it's me in the videos.
11. The FBI is officially "on my trail."

That was it. That was the chain of events that led to my downfall. For all I knew they were listening in on my phone call with my mother. The thought of my phones being tapped really freaked me out. If I was silent on the phone before, well I was even more silent now.

And my mother wasn't done talking. She had a lot more things to tell me. And the things she told me were way more devastating than being caught on video. The things she shared with me would cause me to question everything I had done, everything I ever felt and everything I thought I knew.

Listening to my mother almost drained all the hope I had in my body. Her conversation with me depleted me. When she finished telling me what she needed to tell me I was emotionally shattered.

She said, "Curtis, these people say you might be guilty of federal witness tampering. They say that's punishable by ten years in prison. They told me they have enough evidence right now to bring charges against you. They know where you live, they know where you work and everything about you.

"I told them something must have happened to you for you to do those things. I told them you aint never committed a crime and that you were a good man. And then, well… then I told them something that made them back off you.

"What I'm about to tell you is gonna be hard for you to hear but you need to hear it. It's the reason why the agents aren't banging on your door right now. It is the reason they haven't come to your house to arrest you. And it's also the reason you don't have to worry about them agents anymore. I need you to listen and listen clearly.

"Many years ago, right after I gave birth to your sister the doctors came in and told me and your father that I should never ever try to have any more children. When I was pregnant and carrying with your sister my uterus tore and I was bleeding everywhere. By the time I got to the hospital I had lost a lot of blood and the doctors couldn't stop my bleeding.

"They had to cut your sister outta me and then after that they left all but left me on the table to die. No matter what they tried or how hard they tried, the bleeding wouldn't stop. So they stopped giving me blood to replace the blood I was losing.

221

"Then they say I bled out on that table and that I had officially died. But then something strange happened. Minutes after they declared me dead my vitals somehow came back, and the bleeding stopped. I had somehow come back to life.

"It was a miracle. The doctors say they couldn't explain what happened, but they told me and your father that I could never have any more kids. They say my uterus was too thin and if it tore again, the next time I would surely bleed to death.

"And I was fine with that, but your father wasn't. He always wanted a big family, but I knew I couldn't give him one. And I was sad knowing that. I knew I couldn't give him the family he deserved and unfortunately there was nothing either of us could do about it.

"Then one day about five years later he came home and told me about two twin baby boys that needed to be adopted. He heard about it through a church ministry. There was a young teenage girl who was pregnant, and were babies were being put up for adoption.

"She was only fifteen years old. And not only was she pregnant, but she was pregnant with triplets. Child Services said the mother was too young to care for all three babies. They said it was too big of a responsibility for a fifteen-year-old. They said two of her babies were being put up for adoption and she was gonna be allowed to keep the other.

"So we put in our application to adopt one of her babies.
We were interviewed by all kinds of people. They wanted to make sure we were good parents. They came and inspected our home, they looked at our cupboards to see if we had enough food and looked in our finances to see if we had enough money.

"We never imagined how difficult it would be to adopt a child. But somehow, by the grace of God we got approved. They chose us to be parents. And they told us we were approved to but both babies. We were absolutely thrilled. Our prayers had been answered.

"We named one of the babies Curtis (which is you) and we named the other baby Calvin. The man you went to see in court, well that's your twin brother. That missing juror is your identical twin brother."

At this point I could not believe what my mother was telling me. Calvin was my brother after all. And the story I made up and told the Colombians actually had some truth to it. I wished I could have stopped my mother right there and asked her a few questions, but I couldn't. She wasn't done talking and I vowed to myself that I would listen. So that's what I continued to do.

My mother continued, "Then, after we adopted yall things got really difficult. When the two of you were about nine months old, we received a notice from Child Services that a family member of your birth mother had come forward and wanted to take the two of you from us. They say the babies belonged with their blood relatives and they threatened to take both the twins. Your father and I were devastated. We were heartbroken.

"We couldn't stomach the thought of losing the two of you. We had raised you both since you were infants. And now nine months later some distant relative was trying to take yall from us. And even though we were good parents, we worried that the courts might lean toward sending you both to live with your blood relatives.

"We didn't know what to do. Then one day we got another letter in the mail saying that the family member would settle for us keeping one of the twins and letting them take the other. Fearing we might lose the both of you, we went ahead and signed the papers. We gave away our custody of one of the babies.

"So we kept you and gave them Calvin.
When y'all were born both of your last names were
Wilson. That's your father's last name. But when they took
Calvin from us, his new family changed his name
from Wilson to Lawrence. His name is Calvin Lawrence.

"Years later we learned that the people we signed
Calvin over to weren't even related to him. They were some
rich Black couple who hired a big shot lawyer and tricked us
into signing over Calvin. We wanted to fight it and try to get
him back, but we didn't have the money to hire a good
lawyer.

"Plus, we had already signed all types of papers and
we were always afraid we might lose you too. So we let it go.
We had to. But we knew he was in good hands. His adopted
mother was a teacher, and her husband was a wealthy
businessman. So he was in good hands, albeit crooked
hands.

"And many, many years later when you
were sixteen, we received another letter in the mail. This time
it was a letter from the Department of Family Services. The
letter said that your birth mother had died of an illness and
that the state of Georgia sent its condolences.

"Then the letter said that your siblings were doing well
but because of confidentiality laws their whereabouts would
not be disclosed. It also mentioned that there was no father
listed on your birth certificates and that none of your birth
mothers' relatives were identified in any of their records.

"The letter just went on and on about adoption rights
and confidentiality. It said that it was in the best interest of
all parties that all three siblings remain in separation until
adulthood. They didn't want any of the parents contacting

224

any of the siblings until you all were grown. And we agreed to that when we signed the papers when we adopted you.

"But then the letter got a little confusing. It said that there was a clerical error in the adoption papers. In the records it lists your birth mothers name as Olivia. The records say she birthed triplets at the age of sixteen but because of her age two of her babies were ordered for adoption, and one baby was to remain in her care. The two babies she gave up were you and Calvin, and we initially adopted the both of you.

"But this is where things got interesting. The letter said the clerical error was that they listed three boys in the birth records. Your mother did give birth to three babies, but the error was that it listed all three babies as boys.

"But she didn't have all boys. Only two of the triplets were boys. The other baby was a girl. The baby that your mother was allowed to keep was a girl. A baby girl that she named Diana. Your birth mother's name was Olivia Johnson, and you, Calvin Lawrence and Diana Johnson are all her children. So not only do you have an identical twin brother, but you also have a twin sister as well. She said "Curtis", somewhere out there a massive piece of your heart is waiting to be found."

At this point I was speechless, and an extreme feeling of sadness moved through me. I was devastated, I was lost, and I was alone. By now a steady stream of tears began to fall from my eyes. My mother had no idea, but on the other end of the phone I was silently and painfully crying. I couldn't believe what she just told me. Diana Johnson was my sister. My triplet sister.

The woman I fell in love with and traveled hours and miles to see was my kin. The woman I cherished so dearly that I had a man killed was my sister. How could this be? How did this happen?

For the love of Diana, I orchestrated the murder of my very own brother. My twin brother. I felt worthless.

I couldn't explain the feeling of guilt that passed through me. As my mother spoke, on the other end of the phone I continued to silently weep. I wept uncontrollably. The tears fell so hard and fast that my eyes began to swell. My face was sunken, and my spirit was broken.

How could I have gotten this so wrong? What had happened to me that allowed me to severely misread my message from Diana. I couldn't believe what my ears had been told. I was a worthless and meaningless individual.

After hearing this news, I pitifully ended the conversation with my mother by apologizing to her and telling her that I loved her. I told her it was a lot of information for me to process and I would call her back after I had time to gather myself.

But before I hung up the phone, she apologized to me. She told me the letter about my birth mother's passing came only a year after my father had died. She said she wanted to tell me then, but the timing just didn't seem right.

I told her I loved her and that I understood. And then we both told each other we loved one another again, and then our conversation ended.

As I laid in my bed and processed everything my mother told me, it became clear to me that the dream I had with Diana was not a dream meant for a potential romance. It was a dream for a potential friendship. A long lasting and everlasting friendship.

Never in my dream or in person had I ever been intimate, or even closely intimate with Diana. The only thing she ever allowed me was a hug. We had a natural connection and immediately fell for each another. And we liked each other because we were so much alike.

226

We were of the same genetics. Our chemistry was strong, and it pulled us together. But it was not because of love at first sight, but because we were from the same womb.

We were of the same genetic makeup. This explained why our thoughts and likes were so similar. This explained why we were immediately drawn to each other.

With the power of love, Diana messaged me in my dream and found me. She had somehow pulled me in and given me everything I needed to find her. She gave me her name, and her address, and most importantly she gave me a feeling of love. A powerful feeling, I had never felt before.

The power of Diana's love was extreme, and it did exactly what she intended it to do. It brought both me and Calvin to her. But unfortunately for us, we all misread each other's feeling for one another. And Calvin made the same mistake I made…only his mistake would prove to be fatal.

I would never know how Diana and Calvin met, or how they connected, but I'm sure they found each other much like I found Diana. Not knowing they were siblings, Diana and Calvin courted each other. But ultimately, they were soon pushed apart.

Diana would not allow anything other than a friendship. The pictures at her house of them holding hands didn't mean they were in a relationship. It only meant that they had made a connection. They had formed a liking for each other. But as Calvin tried to get closer, Diana kept him at bay.

I couldn't help but remember the conversation I had with Diana when we first met. When she told me that her mother appeared in her dream and told her that she was not alone, and that one day they would come to her and protect her and love her.

Diana didn't know what her mother meant but now everything was becoming clear. Diana's mother (or should I say our mother) was foreseeing the future. The people who she said would come for her did in fact come. Those people were me and Calvin.

We both came to her. And just as our mother prophesied, both of us came to love and protect her. But the love we sought was much different than the love our mother envisioned.

Not knowing we were siblings, all three of us mistook the powerful feelings we had for one another. Our love was evident but also misguided. And unfortunately, the love that brought us together would ultimately forever keep us apart.

There would be no opportunity for reconnecting. I had done too much. I had destroyed any chance of that ever happening. I had orchestrated the murder of my twin brother and had been shunned forever by my twin sister. I had single handedly destroyed any chance of getting to know two of the most important people in my life.

The only good to come from this was my mother's explanation to the FBI agents of why I had done the strange things they had me on video doing. When the agents pressed my mother for information, she told them the same story she told me. She told them that the missing juror was my identical twin brother.

She told them that when I found out I had a brother I took time off from my job and went to see him. She told them I went there to meet him and that was why I went to the trial every day. She told them I wasn't there to corrupt the jury; I was there to see my brother Calvin.

She told them that was why I was in disguise and that was why I snuck into his hotel room. I was there to secretly spy on my long-lost twin brother. And the agents believed it.

It not only sounded believable, but it was the truth. And that true story was why I hadn't been arrested or even questioned by the police. That true story was why I was sitting alone in my home instead of sitting in a local jail cell. They believed my mother's story. They believed it because it was a very believable, true story.

And at some point, I knew Diana would hear the details of this story as well. She was destined to find out because my story was her story. Our stories were intermingled. I knew one day she would find out about me and find out about Calvin. But the news wouldn't come from me. I wanted no part of delivering it.

My mother would probably be the one to reach out to her. Whether Diana wanted to hear it or not my mother was sure to contact her and tell her the same story she told me. She was good at explaining things. And no one could explain this better than her.

But as for me, I was done. My life was ruined, and I wanted to be alone. I vowed to never speak of Calvin, J3 or Diana ever again. I vowed to never mention the mysterious people I met or the extraordinary incidents I participated in. That part of my life was just a dream. It was nothing more than a beautiful dream about THE EXTRAORDINARY MIND OF AN ORDINARY MAN.

Made in United States
Orlando, FL
25 August 2022

21519948R00127